I0623096

ABANDONED

ARMAND ROSAMILIA

SEVERED PRESS
HOBART TASMANIA

ABANDONED

CHAPTER 1

Daisuke needed his wife to be quiet for a minute so he could get his bearings and make sure they weren't still being hunted.

She whimpered next to him, but he gave her a sharp look he knew conveyed his displeasure.

Kimiko covered her mouth and closed her eyes.

The boat is this way, Daisuke thought, unsure where he was on the island. Could they swim back to the mainland? He didn't think so. It was nine long miles to Nagasaki. In the dark. With turbulent waves crashing and a storm approaching. He knew at his advanced age he'd be lucky to get more than a few swim strokes in before being crashed against the rocks.

They needed to keep moving. The others were all dead. He'd watched as they'd been ripped apart. He watched as…

Something fell close to them, either a crumbling piece of a building or something had been thrown. How strong were these things?

"Come. We need to keep moving," Daisuke whispered to his wife. "We need to find a way off the island."

"We should've never come to this cursed place," Kimiko said loudly. She was crying, her eyes wide and wild. She stared at the towering, dilapidated buildings blocking the moonlight, pressing in above them. "I told you this was wrong on so many levels."

"Nonsense," Daisuke said. "How were we to know?"

Kimiko pointed a finger at her husband. "You knew. We all knew the risk. Your partners told you."

"We didn't know about this. How could we know?" He was about to argue with his wife more when he heard a scraping noise a few levels above them.

It was too dark to see, but he knew what it was. He knew there would be more to follow as well.

Long nails scraping against the cement. Taunting the couple.

Daisuke grabbed his wife by her hand and led her away. They needed to keep moving.

With so much rubble and decay, he knew it was only a matter of time before either of them tripped and went down hard on a block of cement or a spike jutting from the ground.

He'd been a fool. Damn arrogant. Hadn't Akira, his son, told him this was not only going to bankrupt the company, but it would lead to renewed anger and sorry.

The island was the scene of so much tragedy in the history of Japan. The ghosts of the past haunted the eight hundred thousand square feet of the outcropping. Who would've known such evil lurked in such a small area, a supposedly abandoned island that had somehow housed over five thousand coal miners and their families?

Now it was in ruins.

And it would be, because of Daisuke's arrogance, their final resting place.

Kimiko tripped first, dragging Daisuke to the ground with her.

She cried out in pain and rolled over onto the uneven ground, the blood from the gash in her forearm glowing in the slice of moonlight slipping in through empty apartments above.

Daisuke had suffered nothing more than his kneecaps hurting as he'd hit the ground.

The scraping noise was closer, maybe a level lower and still right above them. He knew they were sitting ducks.

"Come, we need to find the boat," Daisuke said, roughly lifting his wife from the ground and dragging her along until she got her feet under her and ran with him.

The island is small. Five hundred feet across, he thought. *Surely we can find the water and follow it back to the gate and the boat*. They had no choice but to keep moving and hope they found a passage to safety.

Six of his coworkers had perished since they'd been on the island. More than people he worked with, though. Friends. Those who stupidly believed Daisuke could turn Forbidden Island around, wipe away the pain it had caused the Japanese, Chinese and Korean people. Build a learning center. Have tours from the mainland. Not shy away from history but try to learn from it.

Mostly, he wanted to get his hands on the rich coal deposits still underneath the island.

The last illegal survey he'd done had shown him what he knew and more: since the operation had been shut down abruptly in April of 1974, nothing had been touched. The equipment, while archaic and in desperate need of replacement, was still in the tunnels. The main passage had been sealed shut. No one had touched a thing in over forty-five years.

Securing the government's trust to move ahead with his plan hadn't been easy. Six years of filing paperwork, shaking hands and bribing a few top officials had taken a toll on his bank account and his health. His wife and son had tried numerous times to talk him out of this. Why hadn't he listened?

Opening the tunnel had been a mistake. One that had cost all of them their lives.

Kimiko groaned as she stumbled again, but he was able to stop her and keep her on her feet.

"It's not too far," Daisuke said. He had no idea where they were. He could hear the waves splashing all around them but couldn't see the ocean past the monolithic buildings.

The only safe way off the island was through the iron gate to the boat landing. Otherwise, it was a thirty-foot plunge off the side into the rock-strewn water, where sand tiger sharks and giant squid might be lurking. Now he wanted to kick himself for not doing his research, thinking he'd never need to worry about what sea creatures might get between him and Nagasaki.

My arrogance is my undoing, Daisuke thought, not for the first time, either. He'd argued his way to the top of the company. Fought against natural energy and solar power. Handed money under so many tables to keep the technology at bay he'd lost count. His partner, who he called The Texan, had helped him along the way. Until he'd double-crossed him. Tried to steal his company out from underneath his feet when he wasn't looking.

None of that mattered now.

The scraping above was so loud it drowned out the waves, even buried his wife's screams now. They were all around them, above and out of sight.

Daisuke turned the next corner, praying the gate was in sight. He frowned. He'd somehow circled back to the mine entrance.

"They're herding us," Kimiko said between her cries. "They want us to go back into the tunnel."

Daisuke shook his head. He was tired of running. Tired of being scared. "No. We make a stand. We go down fighting, Kimiko." He turned to his wife. "I am sorry. I led you to your death."

"You led me to a death with you. If it is our time, so be it." Kimiko took a deep breath and wiped her eyes. "We need to find weapons."

Daisuke smiled. They might get through this. They'd fight their way to freedom. Maybe there weren't as many creatures as he thought. Maybe…

The first one to drop down landed on his wife, claws and blood flying.

It was followed by many more, the chittering and scraping of claws deafening.

CHAPTER 2

Forbidden Island rose from the endless waters, a small blip in a vast ocean. From this view, Akira Higuchi felt like it was at the end of the Earth, even though he knew Nagasaki was close to his back. Nine short miles. To turn and look would be robbing himself of the illusion he was alone.

As the island's features became clearer, Akira shuddered.

This was where his parents had last been sighted.

"Are you sure about this?" Eddie Park, his best friend and business partner, asked. He was standing next to Akira on the rail shaking his head. "This brings back some bad memories."

Akira had to agree. The island had been home to thousands of prisoners during World War II. All working the coal mine for Japan's war machine. He glanced at Eddie, who had even deeper memories: his grandfather had been a prisoner of war on the island, a Korean farmer pulled from his fields to live in squalor and filth. He'd died in the mines, the body never recovered.

7

It was a dark history of Japan Akira knew no one would ever forget. It was also a point of contention between him and his father, who always looked past morals and doing the right thing when there was money to be made.

The fact Eddie was even next to him on this journey spoke volumes.

"Is someone meeting us on the island?" Eddie asked, looking down into the water.

"Yes. I arranged for a guide and the police should be there, too," Akira said. "On one hand, they say it might be a crime scene, but on the other… Forbidden Island is, well… forbidden."

"Yet your father managed to buy it," Eddie said and shook his head. "I wonder if any man or place is beyond your father putting a price on."

"I haven't met or seen it yet." Akira had a love/hate relationship with his parents. They'd treated him to the finest things in life growing up. They'd pampered him. Given him money out of college to start his own company, thinking he'd eventually take over their multiple companies.

Akira had gone against them and had sunk his money into electric cars, solar power and a clean-living concept foreign to his father, who'd made millions off of coal mines, offshore oil rigs and stripping the jungles of trees.

When he'd heard his father had somehow purchased the island, even though it hadn't been used in years and the coal might have been taken from it, which is why it was no longer in use… Akira shook his own head. It made no sense.

No one could definitively say where his parents were now. They'd gone to the island with a team. That much was known. Because of the touchy subject of Forbidden Island, no one in Nagasaki knew what they were doing. His father had quietly rented a boat from a captain who could keep his mouth shut for a pocketful of cash. They'd left nothing behind in the rental, taking their suitcases with them. Everything.

The captain and his boat hadn't been seen since, either. Akira imagined his family were wondering what had happened, and a police inquiry was likely started. With something as delicate as the island, though, Akira thought it would all be swept under the rug.

Forbidden Island loomed only nine miles off the coast, and it was a constant reminder of the tragedies that had happened in the past.

Akira was Japanese by birth, but he'd been sent to New York City as a child and raised by a revolving door of nannies, teachers and mentors. He'd see his parents when they flew in for holidays or his father had business in the city. His mother was always sad, whispering to her only child how she wished his life was different.

Not that Akira could complain too much. He was beyond rich. Pampered. He lived a spoiled life, but a resentful one. He wanted to be a normal kid, with parents who doted on him. Who cared about his studies and interests.

"We have company," Eddie said at his side, bringing Akira out of his dark thoughts.

At first Akira didn't know what his friend was talking about because there wasn't a boat in sight. But as they got closer to the only landing spot, he saw the man leaning against the imposing gate.

"No way," Akira said. "How did he know…"

"That's what The Texan does," Eddie said with a groan. "He's always two steps ahead. That's why your father and The Texan didn't get along. They were one and the same."

Akira stared at the man on the small landing. Dressed in his denim outfit and white cowboy hat, with his long graying beard and beady eyes, he was an imposing figure. Six and a half feet tall and pushing over three hundred pounds on a massive frame, The Texan could scare people into making a deal with him. It was what Akira's father loved about the man and decided to partner with him. Until things went south.

The Texan waved. Akira did not return it.

When the boat stopped next to the landing, The Texan put up a hand.

"Don't bother coming ashore, son. This is my property," The Texan said. He shrugged. "This is also a crime scene. The locals have sealed it off. I can't go any further onto the island just yet."

Akira shook his head. "This island is my father's, not yours. Step aside."

The Texan pulled out a stapled set of papers from his pocket, holding onto them in the breeze. "Court order. As you know, Daisuke and I were still partners in quite a few projects. Including DKA Holdings, which is what Kimiko Island falls under."

Akira was stunned. He'd never heard of DKA Holdings, and apparently his father was renaming the island in his mother's name.

The Texan must've seen the confusion on Akira's face, because his own look softened. "Sorry, kid. I guess it was supposed to be a surprise about the renaming. You can't use the original name, and Forbidden Island sounds more like a bad amusement park ride."

"DKA Holdings?"

Another shrug from The Texan. "One of the many companies we co-owned. Your father added this island to that portfolio so it would fly under the radar. I never agreed to it. I thought it was a waste of a lot of money, but you know your father."

Akira felt like he knew his father less and less. Daisuke owned at least sixty companies, either as sole owner or in partnership with The Texan. Since their falling out over differences as to what they should do going forward, they'd been entrenched in a legal battle for control of the companies. Nothing had been resolved so far, though, and if his parents were dead…

"The judge has sealed everything up nice and tight until your father returns. It was part of the deal. Since he's been gone a week without communication, it falls to me to keep moving along. I can't make changes. I can't sell or buy anything. All I can do is hope for his return with a funny story about where he's been," The Texan said.

"You did this," Akira said quietly. "You knew he'd get most of the businesses because he started them. You knew there was only one way to wrest it from my father."

The Texan narrowed his eyes. "I don't like what you're implying, son. Despite what you think, I love the man. He's made me more money than I can possibly spend. We worked well together… until we didn't. Philosophical reasons. He doesn't care about the environment, and in my old age I was starting to see the folly in tearing up every inch of the planet for fuel." The Texan sighed. "But I didn't do any harm to Daisuke."

Eddie put a hand on Akira's shoulder. "Let's go. We'll contact the lawyers and authority. See what you can legally do."

Akira pointed at The Texan. "This isn't over." He knew he was losing his cool and about to say something he might regret or could be used against him in the future. He turned away and waved for the captain to take them back.

"They're not on the island, kid," The Texan said. "It's been gone over with a fine-tooth comb. There's not a lot of places to hide when you go building to building. If I hear anything, I will let you know."

Akira turned back but Eddie got in his way.

"Let it go. Keep your mouth shut," Eddie said. "Remember what happens when you don't listen to me?"

Akira sighed. "Kris Scarlet. I get it." He refused to look back at the island, staring at the coastline of Nagasaki and wondering what his next step would be to find his parents.

CHAPTER 3

The Texan nodded when he saw Akira staring at him as the boat turned back to the shoreline. While he personally liked the kid, this was business. It had always been about the money and seeking even more money.

"Are they gone, Mister Paisley?"

The Texan sighed. "Give it a minute, Hiro. It isn't a magical flying boat. Relax. Take in the scenery."

"I don't like it on this side of the gate," Hiro Yamada, hidden behind the gate, said, his voice cracking. "It smells like death."

The Texan, who had been named Rutger Paisley, looked at the seagulls overhead. The island didn't smell like death, it stunk like thousands of bird droppings over the years. The place was filthy with it.

He waited an extra three minutes after the boat with Akira was long gone before he unlocked the gate. He had a moment where he smiled and wondered if it wouldn't do Hiro, his assistant, good to spend the night on the supposedly haunted island. He needed to man up and stop being such a coward.

Hiro nearly fell into the water as he rushed past The Texan, who grabbed the little man's shoulder and held him up.

"You don't want to go in that water," The Texan said. "I saw quite a few shark fins as we were talking."

Hiro fell against the gate, closing it. He strained his neck to see into the depths, eyes wide. "Sharks? Really?'

"Oh yeah. All kinds of killers, too. Great white, hammerhead, tiger shark… a dozen different species in these waters, all maneaters," The Texan lied. He had no idea if there was anything in these waters bigger than a goldfish. All he knew about fish was the delicious taste when his crew of chefs prepared them. Unless he could monetize a shark, he couldn't care less.

"I'll call for the boat," Hiro said. He pulled his phone from his pocket. "I recorded your conversation, too. For posterity."

"Erase it." The Texan knew nothing important had been said. Akira hadn't taken the bait to explode and say something stupid to be used against him. He was smarter than he looked. Maybe he was finally realizing the world wasn't so black and white, and his vanity save the world campaign wasn't going to pay his bills. "Hire someone to keep tabs on the kid. I want to know his every move in real time, especially if he stays in Nagasaki or Japan for more than a couple of days."

"Of course." Hiro was still flat against the gate, reluctantly moving a few steps to the side when The Texan locked the gate.

Something awful had gone on inside the gate on the island. Local authorities had found bloodstains. No bodies. No bloody weapons. Nothing to point them in any direction. Of course, once The Texan had arrived, he'd shut it all down. He wanted to make sure nothing escaped into the media. The last thing he wanted was a panic and a focus on Forbidden Island. Now that it was under his umbrella, and until Daisuke popped back up, he'd go ahead with the plans to reopen the coal mine and see if it was worth it.

If not... maybe a luxury island? He could tear down the tenements and toss them into the ocean. Extend the island with a pier for yachts. With it being so small, he envisioned only a few boats at a time. He'd put up one of his The Texan BBQ Joint locations, the first outside the United States, onto the dreary place. A small hotel or some private bungalows. A swimming pool and tiki bar. It would be a super private resort. He'd just need to hide the entrance to the mine so the eyesore wasn't a focus.

"What are you thinking about, sir?" Hiro asked.

"Money. What else?" The Texan saw his boat approaching. "We need to build a team to clean the island. Sweep away the broken toys and the fallen cement. Bring it down to the foundation. Quietly, of course. No use in alerting anyone to the plan."

"And if eyes from the mainland turn in your direction, sir?"

The Texan smiled. "An American dollar and a sizable donation go a long way in this part of the world. Do what needs to be done. Don't get cheap, either. If you get pushback at any point, I want to be included in the exchange."

"As you wish." Hiro hopped onto the boat as soon as it was close enough, helping his boss on next. "Do you envision a timeline? What if the Higuchis are still alive?"

The Texan smiled. "Then we cease operations and I present Daisuke with my master plan and see what he says. If he's not interested and wants to pursue coal mining, so be it. I've sunk my teeth into DKA Holdings. He won't be able to shake me easily. No matter what happens, I'll make money off of this venture. As usual."

By the time they'd pulled into dock, Hiro had things in motion. It would be a week or two before the crew could be set, a barge for debris extraction ordered, power to be run to the island, and a dozen other things The Texan wasn't personally going to worry about. That's why he paid Hiro a ridiculous amount of money: the man could get things done. Hiro was never going to be mistaken for a tough guy, which worked to his advantage. He seemed like the sniveling coward who never made eye contact but get him going on the phone and he became a three hundred pound bodybuilder who lowered his voice and rammed it down your throat.

"I need a stiff drink, a couple of women to distract me, and some good food," The Texan said to Hiro. "I'll be in my hotel room. I need a nap after all of that sun and talking."

The Texan walked to his nearby hotel, noting the three bodyguards fanned out around him, looking for trouble. Not that he thought there'd be any, but it was good to feel safe in a strange city. This had been his first time in Nagasaki, even though he'd done a lot of business over the years in Japan. It's where he found Hiro, working for a rival, and lured him away with not only money but power. Unbeknownst to anyone, especially Daisuke, Hiro Yamada was a silent partner in a few of the smaller businesses. He was rich beyond what a normal man would consider well-off, but it wasn't about the money. The Texan was good in reading people and knowing what made them tick. What they really wanted. Was it money? Power? The ability to feel loved, or to dominate the opposite sex? To be dominated by the opposite sex?

I didn't get to this point by being stupid or feeling lucky, The Texan thought. *I got to where I am because I had the rare combination of intelligence, cunning and the ability to sense a deal before it happened.*

He had no plans to stay more than a night, especially if Akira didn't linger. He'd need to put some distance from himself and Forbidden Island.

Kimiko Island, he thought. *In honor of the fallen woman.*

It would be a good bit of publicity if he shed a fake tear or two during the opening and talked about what a fine and upstanding woman Kimiko had been, both to her family and to the company. Even though The Texan thought the woman too smart for her own good, and with no real sense of humor or personality, it would give a face and sympathy to the project. He'd need to mention Akira as well, in a good light, as if the boy had been a son to him and he would mentor the man in any way possible.

He thought better of it. Akira wouldn't fall in line or go along with it. He might speak out in the press and put a bad light on things, especially the way they were playing out. Would keep playing out.

The Texan got to his room, cranked the air conditioning and stripped down, sliding into bed and closing his eyes with a smile.

Plenty of time to worry about money later, he thought, and was asleep in seconds.

CHAPTER 4

Akira hated doing these talks, but he knew it had to be done. He knew it was as much about him, as the face of the company, doing the actual TEDTalk, as it was the message.

Today, it was a focus on the different types of renewable energy.

The room was filled with two dozen handpicked men and women, all chosen because they'd ask the right questions. Nothing controversial or dramatic. Intelligent enough to give his speech what it needed: relevance and positivity.

In the balcony was the crowd, used to fill out the video feed and make it look like it was a packed house. Akira had marveled at how long it took nearly twenty men and women to get the lights just right, the monitors, the screen, the seats so it looked like hundreds were in the room.

He knew it was a necessary evil. It kept his brand in front of the masses, and he knew brand was a bad word unless you dealt in its currency. If it changed the minds of a few people, it was worth it.

At least that's what he kept telling himself.

"Another packed house," Eddie joked. He looked ridiculous in his striped gray suit and matching Fedora, but Akira wasn't in the mood to bust his friend about it. He was too nervous to try to distract himself. Better to stay focused.

This would be his first appearance since his parent's disappearance, too. It had been four weeks without a word. He'd done his best to stay under the radar, and his team had done an amazing job keeping the news media out of his face. Akira had spent considerable money to find out anything he could, and a score of lawyers to make sure his parent's money wasn't taken.

The Texan, out of generosity or a good publicity stunt, had gone on the record saying he'd never touch anything not also in his name. He'd even split it with Akira, shifting the companies from Daisuke to his only son… but then The Texan had smiled and swore it was only a matter of time before Daisuke and Kimiko were found, taking a break from the stress of their lives. They'd pop up in Paris or the Canary Islands, Canada… where they had a home, smiling and holding hands.

"Sometimes a man and woman need a break to reconnect," The Texan had said and winked. "If you know what I mean." It had become fodder for the tabloids and newscasts, everyone smiling and hoping for the best.

Akira knew his parents were dead. He could feel it. He didn't want their money, and he sure wasn't going to get into bed with The Texan and run companies that stripped the world of their natural resources. He'd do his best to subtly tear them down, though, with everything in his power he had. He'd toyed with the idea, when his parents were eventually found and buried, to use their substantial wealth to oppose everything his father had stood for. Tear it down brick by brick.

His parents were dead. It was inevitable, and Akira needed to steel himself for the closure to it. It wasn't because he was indifferent or had no emotion. He'd learned at an early age to compartmentalize his feelings. He'd learned it from his father.

Akira stepped onto the stage and plastered a smile on his face, bowing low and feeling the energy of the applause. He knew some of it was being pumped in through the speakers, and more might be added in the trailer when it went 'live' with a two-minute delay, in the event there was a glitch or Akira stumbled during the hour and fifteen-minute presentation.

He'd rehearsed it so many times he could probably do it in his sleep, but this was going to be the important and last time. At least, he hoped it was going to be the last one he had to do.

Akira hit all the marks, stepping across the stage, pointing at the screen behind him, pausing at his set jokes so the audience could laugh, and a couple of dramatic pauses as he showed startling footage of oil-engulfed birds, seals and whales. Dead fish washed ashore was another sight that brought a few gasps from the crowd, and Akira smiled inside. The people needed to be aware of what was happening.

He never mentioned his father's many companies by name, or anyone else. It was decided in the initial meetings Akira could still have impact without pointing a finger at a specific company. They were all guilty and lumping them together was easy enough without name-dropping.

Halfway through his six steps to renewable energy, while talking at length about hydro energy, Akira stepped to his left as the crowd watched a quick twenty second clip above and behind him, getting ready for his next point and knowing where the camera would be focused on.

Eddie was near the curtain and staring up at the balcony.

Akira followed his gaze and frowned.

"You're frowning," the producer said in his earpiece. "Stop frowning."

Akira stopped frowning, but inside he'd wanted to scream.

Kris Scarlet, his former girlfriend, was standing near the exit in the balcony, and staring at him. A blank expression on her face, which he'd used to think was funny but now knew meant she was unreadable. Always unreadable.

"Focus," the producer said. "Three... two... one..."

Akira dove back into the presentation, never openly missing a beat. He was proud of himself when he stepped off the stage to wild applause. He punched Eddie in the arm backstage.

"What's that for? Did you notice who was in the audience?" Eddie asked, rubbing his arm.

"I punched you because you distracted me," Akira said. "Why'd you do that? It almost threw me for a loop."

The conversation was stopped when everyone came to congratulate him, the producer rushing in from the trailer and giving Akira a hug and mentioning awards and working together again in the future.

Akira took it all in with a smile, but he wanted to get away. Back to the hotel and a quiet dinner from room service, followed by some emails and the news before going to bed. They'd leave before dawn to get out of New York City. He needed to fly back to Los Angeles for a meeting.

He knew none of that was going to happen now. Kris was going to follow him to the hotel and make her presence known when Akira was alone. Especially when Eddie wasn't around, who had seen through her deceit and drama from the beginning.

"I'm going to stay with you tonight," Eddie said. "Make it known we're hanging out, if you know what I mean."

Akira shook his head. "She'll scale the side of the building and hide in the shower. Jump out when I go to the bathroom alone."

"Then..." Eddie laughed. "Nah. She can meet you there. I'm not following. I remember college and living with you and your various smells."

"You should talk." Akira looked around but the crowd had dispersed and he was led to the back alley and his waiting limo. He knew she wasn't going to approach in public. For a moment he thought about changing plans and heading straight to the airport, but Kris had always been a step ahead of him. She'd be seated on the plane with a smile when he got on.

"I'll be right next door," Eddie said. "I guess it would be no use to tell the staff to be on the lookout for her and not let her on the elevator. Kris has a way of getting to you no matter what. She'd crawl through a minefield full of sharks in order to ruin your day."

"Why are there sharks in a minefield? Is the minefield underwater, or are the sharks flipping out because they're out of water?" Akira asked, feeling better as the limo pulled into traffic.

Akira was rushed through the lobby. Glancing around, he didn't see her. Up the elevator and onto the top floor and down the hall.

"Are you sure you're good? I can stand guard outside," Eddie said. He shrugged. "Maybe get a chair and sit."

"While you're gone to get a chair, she's going to get inside." Akira smiled. "I guess I need to face her again at some point." He swiped his key card and opened the door. "Besides, she's probably inside already."

Eddie walked away and Akira waited until his best friend was at his own door and entering.

Akira had seen the light on and knew he had turned it off when he'd left that morning.

"Hello, Akira," Kris said, sitting on the edge of the bed. She patted the spot next to her. "We need to talk."

CHAPTER 5

Akira must've looked like a deer in headlights, because Kris laughed and put her hands up. "I just want to talk. I promise. No games. I'm not here to dredge up our past. I'm here to talk about your father."

"What about my father?" Akira asked. He walked around to the desk, keeping as far away from her as possible. He felt like he was in a cage with a lion, and he couldn't turn his back on the beast.

"I haven't heard from him in too long," Kris said. "I'm worried The Texan did something to him."

Akira balled his fists and stared at her. A million questions came into his head at once, but he knew he needed to maintain his cool. "How did you get into my room?"

"Money. Isn't that how we get in everywhere?" Kris stood. She was wearing a black cocktail dress, her hair and makeup perfect. Her stiletto heels were near the desk. She'd made herself at home while she waited for him. "I hacked Eddie's phone, actually. He should be more careful. A stalker could've had your week's itinerary and killed you at a few places."

"Is that why you're here? To kill me?" Akira asked.

Kris laughed again. She looked down at the tight dress. "Where would I hide a weapon?"

"Tell me what you need to and then leave. Permanently," Akira said.

"Trust me, Akira, I had no wish to see you again," Kris said. "Especially after how we left off last time."

There had been a fight. A shouting match. Broken lamps and picture frames, glass covering the living room. If they'd lived in a city or condo and not on sixteen secluded acres, the police would've been called by a neighbor.

"You cheated on me," Akira said.

Kris nodded. "We're bad for each other. Too much passion and too many peaks and valleys. I'm never going to settle down and have children. Never going to have dinner on the table when you get home from a long day at the office. I'm not wired that way. I need excitement. The rush and the drama."

"I thought I could change you," Akira said.

"So did your father."

Akira was across the hotel room and inches from her face before he had time to think. "What does that mean?"

"I've been working for your father for the past four months," Kris said. She wasn't backing down, staring back at Akira. She never backed down. "Mostly doing his grunt work in Texas, Chicago and Jacksonville. Making sure things are running smoothly while he's busy acquiring more companies and trying to get this coal mine up and running."

"You're sleeping with my father," Akira said, the words like bile in his mouth.

"I'm his property manager. I handle certain *affairs*," Kris said.

"You're his whore."

Kris slapped Akira so hard across the face he thought she'd knocked a tooth out. He stumbled back a step but recovered. It knocked some of the fight out of him, too.

She acted like nothing had happened, sitting back down on the bed. "Your parents were supposed to spend a few hours on the island and then head to dinner in Nagasaki to meet with potential vendors. He wanted to fly under the radar and start the work before anyone noticed, hoping a running start and a lot of cash handed under the table would let him get it done."

"As usual, my father doesn't think about ethics or legal matters when it comes to his money." Akira sat down on the bed but away from Kris.

"You always hoped, as he got older, he'd mellow out and see his mistakes," Kris said. "Except it was never a mistake to him. He wasn't worried about the environment or the human race long-term. He was worried about himself, and he never hid from it. He never acted like he wanted to be anything but what he is. You have to give him props for that, at least."

"I always cringe when he donates money to some bogus environmental outfit, claiming they were going to save wildlife or the whales or Bigfoot or something." Akira shook his head. "Only to find out through an easy dig of the company the money was being funneled back to his oil or coal or more than likely a Senator or higher up the food chain. No one called him on it and no one could actually prove it. I know I tried."

Kris nodded. "I remember when you confronted him once. He laughed at you. The man was brazen and bold but careful. He never did anything to put himself in the line of fire. In an alternate reality, your father was a Mob boss."

"I'm not so sure he isn't one in this life," Akira said. "He runs it like The Family in New Jersey. There were always whispers about him working with them, especially on the docks, real estate and I know he purchased a huge tract of land in the Pine Barrens."

"I knew your father's itinerary. There were no vacation plans, no break from business. Your mother was along because some of the irons in the fire had to do with her. She was going to start a couple of small businesses in and around Nagasaki. In her name. They had a full week scheduled," Kris said.

"The Texan blocked me from the island," Akira said. "I think he did something to my parents." He looked at the wall. "Do you think he'd stoop so low?"

They were quiet for a few minutes.

"Do you think your father would do something like that?"

Akira didn't answer, but they both knew the answer: he very well might if he knew he'd get away with it and it would benefit him. Akira's father was not one of the good guys.

"The answer is on the island," Kris said. "I tried to locate the boat captain, but he never returned. Neither did the boat."

"Maybe they took the boat and decided to blow everything off for a few days. Make people worried," Akira said, knowing it rang hollow. His mother was submissive so she'd never be able to sway her husband to do such a thing, and no way he'd think of it. His life was always and only about making money.

"I feel like we're missing something," Kris said.

Akira turned back to her. "What's in this for you?"

She shrugged and it was her turn to look away. "The job." She shook her head. "Ties to your family. To the only real stability I've ever had, even if it was going to be a short-term thing."

"Why didn't you tell me you were working for him? Why didn't he?"

Kris sighed. "I told him not to. It was part of the deal we had. I didn't want you losing your mind or thinking I was stalking you. Getting in with your father for ulterior reasons. I needed work. Money. A new challenge. How many times did I offer to work for you? I'm a damn good property manager and so much more, Akira."

The knock at the door wasn't unexpected, but Akira wondered why it had taken so long.

"That must be Eddie," Kris said and stood, smoothing out her dress and giving Akira a nice view of her butt. "Time to be on my way."

Akira didn't know what else to say. Seeing her again, talking about his father… it was a lot to digest. A part of him hoped he'd never see her again, but, if he was being honest, he hoped he would.

"If you hear anything, please let me know. I'll do the same," Kris said and opened the door. She smiled at Eddie. "How's it going? Did you lose weight, Eddie? You look good. I hope our boy here isn't working you too hard."

Akira stared at Kris as she walked down the hallway to the elevator. Eddie was also checking her out.

"She's a beautiful woman hiding the devil," Eddie said. "How'd she get to you, anyway?"

Akira asked for Eddie's phone and dropped it on the ground. He stepped on it.

Eddie groaned.

"You need a better phone with better security," Akira said. "I need a break to think."

CHAPTER 6

Rutger Paisley took off his cowboy hat and wiped his brow with the back of his hand. He was sweating in his office. "Hiro? Turn up the air conditioning. It's too warm." He glanced out his office window and saw the latest guests taking advantage of his hospitality, riding his prized horses like they were a bunch of toy horses you rode at the front of the grocery store, like he'd done as a kid.

One of those horses was worth everything inside a grocery store, and he was going to put his foot down. Just as soon as Hiro answered him. "Hiro? Where are you?"

His phone rang and he answered before it rang again.

"Sir... did you call for me?" It was Hiro.

Rutger groaned. "Where are you? I've been calling and calling. I need you to do something for me."

"I'm outside, trying to get your guests off of your horses," Hiro said. "I assure you I didn't authorize this."

Rutger smiled. This was why he paid Hiro such a big salary. The man was on top of things. "Be nice about it. They're my sister's kids and families. Buncha idiots, the lot of them. It's because of the moron she married and bred with. Awful trashy people. Have them go to the shooting range. Maybe they'll kill one another and be done with it."

"As you wish, sir," Hiro said.

"Then come up to my office and figure out why it's so hot in this room," Rutger said. "I'm trying to work."

"The makeup team will be here in about an hour," Hiro said. "You have an interview with *Texas Heritage Entrepreneur* today. They're looking forward to it. The editor just called, as if I need reminding. She said they're going to call the spread 'The Texan In Power' or something along those lines."

He smiled again. These days, only his mama called him by his birth name. Everyone else called him The Texan, and he loved it. How many great men had been born and raised in this great State? Dozens. Both former Bush Presidents. Willie Nelson. Dwight D. Eisenhower. Howard Hughes. Larry Hagman. Oliver North and Nolan Ryan. Were any of those great men called The Texan? Not a one.

The article would be quite flattering. They'd talk about all of his work within the community. His rags to riches story he never grew tired of telling. His work with the families of his workers and the money he'd given to the area schools as well as his animal shelters and feeding the homeless once a month through his restaurants.

The Texan wasn't ever worried about an attack or too many hard questions, since he owned the media: both newspapers, the five closest radio stations, the TV station and seven magazines. Hiro was working on these podcast things, too. If there was a voice capable of speaking to the masses, he wanted to own it and have them telling the masses how wonderful he was.

His phone rang and he answered.

"Uh, The Texan, sir… Mister Texan? I'm not sure how to address you, uh, sir." It was his foreman on Forbidden Island.

Kimiko Island, The Texan reminded himself. "How's it going?"

"Well… we're a little behind, to be honest. This is quite a mess. The demo of these buildings will take us months. Months. We're limited to the tools we have, and… some of the men are getting freaked out." Frank hadn't seemed like a negative man when The Texan had hired him and his boys, but maybe he'd been wrong.

"Why? Don't they like their paychecks?" The Texan asked, knowing they all did. The team had been assembled in Texas, paid four times the going rate for this grunt work, and the hotel they were all staying at had been purchased by The Texan so no one else would get close to them. They even had a private chef and two drivers to take them from the boat to the hotel.

"Of course they like their pay, sir, it's just… this island is creepy when the sun starts to drop, to be honest. I'm wondering if we can break an hour earlier. Arrive an hour earlier, too," Frank added quickly.

The Texan sat back in his chair. He started to put his boots up onto the desk but stopped. His desk cost more than most folks' houses, and it was a bad habit. His mama would've rolled over in her grave if he'd put his boots on the furniture.

"I think we have enough men for the job, especially since it's close quarters once you get into the streets, with all the debris," Frank said, taking The Texan's pause for something negative, other than the boss was thinking about his boots, furniture and mama.

"Hold on… you're saying the project is delayed. By how much do you estimate? Give me a real answer and not what you think I want to hear," The Texan said. He never wanted to get the runaround. He'd rather be told the honest truth about it and then deal with it, rather than wasting time.

Frank didn't answer right away, which The Texan took for a good sign. The man's initial answer would've been too positive, too unrealistic. The Texan waited for the real answer.

"If we pick up the pace, and we can somehow sneak a barge to the far side of the island, we might only be ten days behind schedule. That will depend on the weather and what obstacles we encounter," Frank said. "More men might help once we can clear a building down, but without heavy machinery… this is old school, sir. Breaking down walls with sledgehammers starting at the top floor. And…"

Frank sighed.

The Texan smiled and didn't say a word. It was best to let the man work it out on his own. He raised his legs to put his boots on the desk and stopped himself.

"We found a nursery, sir. Rotting cribs and dirty toys on the floor. It was really creepy. The people who lived here left in a hurry. We found moldy plates on tables. Clothing still on hangers in closets falling apart." Frank sighed again. "In one of the buildings we found animal bones. At least, I hope they're animal bones. Picked clean. Hundreds of them. I know there were birds and maybe a dog or cat left behind. Really creepy."

"I'm sure it was. Shovel it all over the side if you haven't already. I'll have a barge out in three days and park it on the far side, like you said. The first load should be all of the incidentals. The toys and furniture. Clear out the buildings, pile and tarp it up. I'll have a second barge in five days. That should give you enough time to fill the first one. Sound like a plan, foreman?"

"It does," Frank said. "What about working an hour earlier each day?"

"I'm paying you boys by the hour and overtime for anything over forty," The Texan said. "Start ninety minutes early and stay ninety minutes later each day. One day off a week on a rotating schedule so there's work always being done. Send Hiro a schedule by the morning."

"Ninety extra minutes in the morning is fine, sir, but… if we stay an extra hour and a half at the end of the shift, it will be dark by the time we leave," Frank said.

"I need this island cleared. I thought when I hired you and your crew, you understood it."

"We do understand, it's just… this island. There's something wrong with it. Something off. You know? It feels like the shadows are creeping in on us." Frank waited for an answer but The Texan let the man stew for a full minute before he answered.

"Until you're back on schedule, these are the hours. I'll send six more men on the barge. That should help, too," The Texan said. "Now, what do you think about the mine entrance? Can we permanently seal it, or no?"

"I think we can," Frank said. "It's closed but it would take a massive amount of work to truly seal it. I'm thinking we can put a facade up in front of it. Build it into the structure of whatever will eventually go in the spot. Tear down everything around it. Whatever you need me to do."

"I need you to get back on track and clear the island before the locals start asking too many questions and it grinds to a halt. Is that understood, foreman?"

"Yes, sir," Frank said.

The Texan disconnected and turned in his chair, staring out the window. He didn't care if the island seemed creepy. Spooky. Heck, if there were ghosts on the big rock he might be able to use it to his advantage, especially at Halloween time.

His thoughts of making money were broken when he saw one of his relatives, maybe a niece, gallop past his window on a horse worth more than she'd make in a lifetime.

The Texan decided to worry about his closer problems.

CHAPTER 7

Frank Meyer needed a drink. Badly. He looked up at the unyielding sun and shook a fist at it, which some of his crew saw and quietly laughed.

They probably think I'm losing my mind, Frank thought. *I probably am losing my mind, come to think of it. The sooner we can get this phase done, the sooner I can get off this rock and get back to civilization. A bar and some Japanese women. Sake. A good cigar. A couple of friendly locals who had no idea what I was saying, and I wouldn't care what they were talking about.*

He walked to the edge of the island and spat off the side. He was thirsty.

"Are you alright, boss? You seem…" Tim Buda, his second in charge, shrugged his shoulders. When Frank stared at him, Tim smiled and wiped his hands on his jeans. "You seem distracted today. What's up?"

"I'm sick of this place. Three weeks is like three years." Frank looked at the men nearby and waved his hands. "Get to work. No breaks. I want to get off of this island before the sun goes down."

"We all do," Tim said. He looked over the edge and shook his head. "Water, water, everywhere, nor any drop to drink."

Frank groaned. "You're not impressing me with your lame quotes. Take your college degree and get back to work. We need to either figure a way to completely block the tunnel or a way to build over it without a problem. In the next three hours." He looked at the sun again. "We're already behind and the locals are going to ask too many questions."

There were also fishing boats nearby, and he didn't think for a second they were simply looking for fish. They were fishing... for information. The Texan had warned him not to talk to anyone. They had a small ten-man crew for the initial work. No sense having a barge anchored with power equipment run by fifty men. Not yet.

Frank hadn't told anyone about his full conversation with The Texan. He'd keep acting like everything was fine. When he'd explained to the men they needed to get up an hour earlier and work, they hadn't complained. They didn't mind being on the island in the daytime, but he knew they'd mutiny if he said they absolutely needed to stay when the sun went down.

It was a feeling he couldn't shake each day, either.

He'd gone against the wishes of The Texan, telling his crew they needed to pick up the pace and get the demo work done or else they *might* have to work later each day. It had not gone over well, to say the least.

The barge would arrive sometime overnight and they'd begun switching from simple demolition to gathering all of the discarded items into a central area near the far side of the island. Already, the pile was too massive for one barge. He toyed with the idea of tossing some of it into the ocean but knew it would eventually wash ashore and create a stir. Better to ask The Texan for another barge for the rest of it.

"Hey, uh, Frank, I got a question." It was one of the men, Chuck Edler, a burly guy with a full beard who loved to climb to the top of the building without worrying about harnesses. He yelled every strike of the sledgehammer until Frank had put an end to it. They were trying to be quiet and do their work, not announce across the water they were here.

"What's up?" Frank asked. He was surprised to see Chuck not above his head somewhere busting out walls.

"I think I found a skeleton." Chuck looked up and down the street. "On the third floor. It's pretty torn up, too. Like animals had gotten to it. Ribs cracked and the skull is fractured. It's definitely human, though."

Frank sighed. He'd been sighing too much so far on this job. Despite the great money, he was having second thoughts. This was not what he'd signed up for. Hazard pay is great until there's a hazard.

"Did you tell anyone else?" Frank asked.

"Nope." Chuck grinned. "Wanted to tell you first. I took a few pics of it on my phone, though."

"Delete them," Frank said. "Show me."

Chuck led Frank to the far building down the block. No one else was working on this one. Chuck liked to work on his own, and most guys let him do whatever he wanted. He was an ironman when it came to demo work, one of the best in Texas. He never took breaks and always had a grin on his face when he was destroying walls, ceilings and floors. He was reckless but hadn't gotten hurt in his career yet. His drinking after the day's end was legendary, too. Frank had once tried to go toe to toe with Chuck and had literally passed out under the table while Chuck finished another bottle of bourbon.

The skeleton was in worse shape than Frank thought it would be. Scattered bones across the cement floor, the spine across the doorway to the room.

Frank bent down. He had seen enough dead animals over the years of clearing houses and lots to know this wasn't an old skeleton. There were bite marks on the bones but no real discoloring. He knew the bones would be stripped clean if this was a body from the mass exodus in 1974.

These bones looked newer. Scraps of skin and clothing on a couple of them.

"Look at the cracked bones," Chuck said. "Like whatever did this sucked out the marrow. Disturbing and kinda cool. Right?"

Frank shook his head. "Not cool at all. Definitely disturbing, though." He stood and paced the room, looking at the bones. This was bad. Really, really bad. If he told anyone, it would shut them down. Not that anyone would know, unless Chuck got drunk and bragged about it.

Chuck was smiling like always, taking it all in again. As if he hadn't already seen it.

"You can't tell anyone about this," Frank said. "I'm serious. This will close us and that means no more pay. No more overtime. The chef and the nice hotel digs are gone." He paused because it didn't look like Chuck was getting what he was saying. "It also means no more good alcohol. Top shelf stuff goes away."

Chuck's smile faltered. "Hey, boss, I'm not going to tell anyone. Relax. It's all good. You can count on me."

"Can I? Drunk Chuck is Loud Chuck. Talkative Chuck. If this gets out…" Frank shook his head again. "No one can know about this. I'm serious. Do me a favor and sweep it all up. We need to hide it until we can get rid of it."

"If we put Bernie on the barge, he might be seen," Chuck said. "We could toss him into the ocean."

Frank frowned. "Who's Bernie?"

Chuck was grinning again. He swept his hand out. "Bernie. I named him."

"Of course you did." Frank knew calling The Texan would make this all worse. Plus, he'd tell Frank to toss the bones into the water and forget about it. "Did you check the rest of the floors and other buildings?"

"I can if you want," Chuck said. "Lots of bird skeletons. Lots of bird droppings, too. I'll do a sweep after I get rid of Bernie."

"Do it quickly and quietly," Frank said. "If you can get to the end of this job, I have a special treat I was going to share with my best workers. A bottle of Pappy Van Winkle bourbon."

"Wow. Nice. It's on my bucket list to try," Chuck said. He acted like he was zipping his mouth closed.

Frank didn't bother telling Chuck The Texan had promised a bottle to every man who did well, from his own personal stock. It would have to be enough to bribe Chuck to keep his mouth shut and help Frank get through this job, which was becoming more and more upsetting.

CHAPTER 8

Kimiko woke in the dark and immediately wished she hadn't. Her body ached. She was thirsty and hungry. The stench of rotting meat was overpowering. Before she could cover her mouth, she was puking.

A low growl echoed from the distance and she tried to relax but couldn't. The acid taste in her mouth made her gag.

Where was Daisuke? She thought she'd been talking to him, but maybe it had been a dream. Her eyes were useless. She wondered if she wasn't in impenetrable darkness and she was blind. The black was so absolute. When she put her finger less than an inch from her eyes, she couldn't see it. Not even a shadow.

Her senses were sharp now. She could hear when they got close to her and when they dropped the tin dish near what she figured was the way from the room. After the first time they'd tried to feed her a dead, raw rat, she'd freaked out and yelled for them to at least cook it and they'd actually listened.

They were smart. They understood her words.

Japanese words, she thought. It made sense. These creatures had likely been a part of the island. Maybe they were originally from Japan.

Maybe they used to be human.

Whatever their origin, they understood and obeyed her when it came to food.

Every other meal, which she figured was once per day, had been cooked.

Kimiko didn't want to know what she was eating most days. The water they gave her in a cracked bowl was tinged with coal, and she knew she was swallowing a lot of it. What could she do?

She'd tried to leave but the growls a few feet from the exit to her cell stopped her each time. Kimiko was being watched. They could see her but she couldn't see them.

Her space was fifteen feet by fifteen feet. Carved walls. Dusty. A caustic smell. She knew she was surrounded by coal and gravel, the floor hard and awful to sleep on.

Where was Daisuke? She'd called out to him, but then the growling started again. The first time she didn't stop, yelling for her husband and for help, she'd been struck in the head and knocked out.

They can see me but I can't see them, Kimiko reminded herself. She had been counting the days by the food left, but then she started to fear they were feeding her at irregular intervals. Was she getting one or two meals a day? She didn't know. A minute could seem like an hour, and she knew she was slowly losing her mind. She'd put her back to a cold wall and close her useless eyes and dream of better times. She slept occasionally, but she had no idea for how long.

Why hadn't they killed her yet? The others were all dead. She'd watched them die. Ripped apart by dark talons, bodies flayed open.

She knew she was deep underground. How far did the mine shaft go? Where was the exit to light and freedom? Would she ever see Daisuke or Akira again?

At the thought of her son, she began to cry. *If I'd only been stronger, more caring, more understanding of him*, Kimiko thought. *He's grown into a strong man despite what we did to him. Not because we showed him the right way, but because he rebelled against our greed and lack of empathy toward the planet.*

Kimiko knew their plans were short-sighted and doing irreparable damage to the Earth. She'd spoken up about it to Daisuke in the beginning, when they'd first tasted the power and money, but she'd stopped. He wasn't listening, anyway.

Her time was spent buying bigger and bigger homes and decorating them. Then she'd grow bored and find another. She had so much jewelry a dozen safe deposit boxes in a dozen different cities didn't put a dent in what she had at hand. She'd forgotten about most of it because it was a constant need to buy more and more.

Daisuke had been having affairs for years, but she turned a blind eye because she was afraid to lose her place in society. Afraid to go back to living like a commoner. She'd become obsessed with the power and the glory. With being in the newspapers, interviewed in magazines and on television. She counted Presidents and celebrities as her friends, although most of it was for show.

Kimiko was startled by a noise nearby and realized she'd fallen asleep at some point. Was it time for another meal or water?

A rustling came from her left and right. She couldn't see but she could feel the space of her room being filled. Was this it? They were finally coming to kill her?

She curled up into a ball, trying to press herself into the hard wall.

Kimiko gasped when her leg was yanked and she was dragged across the floor, her head banging several times as she was moved. Multiple hands on her body now, talons stroking her skin and making her wince.

If they're going to kill me, do it already, she thought. *Save me from this new indignity. Let me go or stop this madness.*

There was grunting now, close to her head. At least three of them, making clucks and clicking noises with their tongues. The monsters had their own language.

At least a dozen hands had touched her body and the smell of so many in such a small area made her gag. She turned her head and felt the bile rising in her throat, the acid burning as it forced its way into her mouth.

Kimiko coughed and spat it out, retching as she turned onto her side.

Her sudden movement and throwing up brought some howls from the creatures around her. She didn't care. The smell was overpowering. She hadn't noticed it before. It was more like a faint sour smell. She realized it was always around, in her nose and mouth constantly. She'd been getting used to it, but now she threw up again.

A loud growl quieted the group, including Kimiko. In the darkness, with nothing to concentrate on, it was deafening. She didn't know if they took a step back from her, but she felt more space.

Her face was grabbed and she let out a scream.

The creature's hands were massive and she could feel the hair and grooves in the skin. She imagined them as black ape hands ending in wickedly sharp claws.

Kimiko tried to turn her head away but it was no use. She didn't possess ten percent of what this creature had in strength, and she knew it wasn't even using a lot of it.

She stiffened when it began sniffing her, inches from her face.

Then the hand was removed as quickly as it had grabbed her, and she felt a trickle of blood on the side of her face.

Kanojo wa toshi o tori sugite imasu, one of them growled quietly.

Then they were gone, leaving Kimiko. She felt the air swish as they moved away from her.

Kimiko began to sob. She didn't know what they were going to do with her now.

She is too old.

Kimiko shuddered despite the warmth of the coal mine and wondered what she was too old for, and if it was a good or bad thing.

CHAPTER 9

Akira traded in a favor or two to get the information, and he knew he'd be in trouble if he showed his hand as to where it had come from. Even though his company was in direct opposition to what his father and The Texan were doing, there were still plenty of people who drifted between the two philosophies. Especially when there was money to be made talking out of both sides of their mouth.

He'd owe a favor or two back in the future. That's how it worked.

"You do have some of your father in you," Eddie said and put his hands up when Akira stared at him. "I'm just saying... whether you want to hear it or not. Your old man might be a callous jerk and unbearable as a dad, but he's still my hero. He built his empire from scratch. He didn't have too many missteps, either. From a purely business outlook... Akira, he's a genius."

Akira had to agree, although he knew his father cut too many corners. Handed off too much cash under the table. Didn't worry about the people or the communities he might interrupt or destroy thanks to his unyielding push for the almighty dollar.

"I'm wondering what I can do to block these plans," Akira said. "If my father and mother are still alive…"

Their original plan for the island was simple: reopen the coal mine and strip it as quickly as possible before the world knew what they were doing. It was a cocky and bold move, especially in today's day and age, where everything was being filmed, either with surveillance cameras or your phone. A plan this audacious could only work if a lot of bribe money was being paid out. Akira was sure it had been or his father would've abandoned it. As much as Daisuke Higuchi might fall in love with a concept, if it made no sense financially, he could easily walk away.

There is always another deal on the horizon, his father had told a young Akira. *You just need to cut your losses and be the first in line for the next one.*

Akira had used this advice for his own companies, although he'd usually walk away when he knew it could potentially hurt the environment. He had to admit, though, a few times it was about money, too.

"They are alive," Eddie said.

"The Texan wants to build a resort on Forbidden Island. A tourist trap." Akira shook his head. "Can you imagine? The locals will be up in arms."

Eddie put up a finger. "He's not stupid. He'll sink a ton of money into the local economy. Hire people from the mainland to work there. He'll need boats to ferry the tourists back and forth. Have the food catered in or however he'll do it. The small towns up and down the coast will be scrambling to strike a deal with The Texan, and he'll give them just enough to keep them happy and out of his business."

"It makes no sense."

Eddie shook his head. "It all makes perfect sense. Your father did the hard part already: paying people for their silence. The Texan swoops in and keeps the cash flow going, but the initial payouts were likely massive. Do you think he really cares if it does great business or it fails?"

"No." If the plan sunk, it was a tax write-off in a foreign country for The Texan. He could fold the losses into several of his other businesses. No matter what he did, he'd come out with more money in the end. He was smart, like Akira's father. They were ruthless when it came to earning, and they knew every loophole imaginable. A lot of times they created their own.

"I know you want to go to Nagasaki and confront The Texan," Eddie said.

"I am and I need you to book my flight."

"No," Eddie said and smiled. "I'll go. If something goes south, you don't want to be in the crossfire. It's best you stay here and continue your work. Besides, you have two conferences in the next week. Another walkthrough for a TEDTalk as well."

Akira narrowed his eyes. "I didn't agree to another one."

"Technically, no… but the deal you signed gave them first right to do another if it was financially worth it. Didn't you see the numbers I emailed you? It was definitely worth it." Eddie laughed. "You're too popular for your own good."

"You're not going," Akira said. "I need you here, now more than ever. You're going to run interference for me so I can get my personal work done. I've touched the tip of the iceberg with The Texan and my father's holdings. I need to do more research, and that involves more favors only I can get."

"Then we continue to monitor the situation from a distance?" Eddie asked.

Akira shook his head. "I have a plan."

Eddie nodded slowly.

Instead of telling Eddie what the plan was, he waved his hand. "Don't you have actual work to do?"

"Seriously, you're not going to fill me in?"

Akira chuckled. "It's a need-to-know basis. Right now, you need to know what my next meeting is and make sure I have everything I need for it."

Eddie shrugged and went to the office door. He stopped and snapped his fingers. "Kris."

"Who?" Akira tried not to smile. Eddie knew him better than anyone.

Eddie came back inside the office and put his hands on the desk. "Please, for the love of all that is holy, tell me you're not getting her involved."

"You worry about my itinerary and I'll worry about my personal life," Akira said, hearing the edge in his voice. He knew he was making a mistake, but he didn't know what other options he had. If he couldn't be in Nagasaki and working with the locals to gain information, who better than Kris? She had a vested interest in this, too. She was working for his father. She wanted answers as well. It made perfect sense.

Except Akira knew it didn't. He had a sinking feeling Kris had moved on from him for bigger fish, and that fish was his father. It was disgusting on so many levels, but mostly... it hurt his pride. He'd loved her. Wanted to spend the rest of his life with Kris Scarlet and make her his wife. Maybe have children together, although the one time he'd brought that up she'd laughed and run her hands down her body.

"Do you know how many hours a day it takes just to maintain this figure? Children stretch your skin. They mess up your insides, too. Ruin this body? Nothing is worth that," Kris had said. He didn't ask if she was joking or being over the top, because he hoped she wasn't serious.

"I'll hire someone to go," Eddie said. "A private investigator. An old white guy wearing a trench coat and fedora. He'll have one of those cheesy moustaches and talk like he's living in the Roaring Twenties."

Akira laughed. "I'm sure an overweight white guy will blend right in."

"Who said he was overweight?" Eddie asked.

Akira waved his hands. "Get out of my office. I'm paying you to work. I'll handle it."

"Please don't do anything stupid, or let her get inside your comfort zone again, Akira. She's bad news. You know it. I know it. She definitely knows it. Don't put a square peg in a round hole, or whatever the saying is." Eddie sighed and stood back up. "I worry about you. Not as my boss, but as my friend."

"You have nothing to worry about," Akira said. "Now go."

Eddie left, shaking his head one last time as he closed the door behind him.

Akira stared at his phone for ten minutes, wondering if he was making the right decision.

Am I doing this because I need her to help with this, and there's no one else in the entire world who can do this job? Is it because I can't stop thinking about her since she broke into my hotel room? I need to stop and think. Take some time to work it out, Akira thought.

That lasted another minute before he called Kris.

CHAPTER 10

Chuck took a swing with his sledgehammer and laughed when the rest of the wall toppled to the ground below. This was man's work, sweet and simple. No giant wrecking balls, which could topple a building in minutes. He could feel his arms burning and his breathing ragged under his mask.

He'd started on the top floor and had already knocked a hole in two of the four walls, careful not to bust out the corner supports and have the cement roof fall and crush him. It took a refined skill to take a building down with only a sledgehammer and not fall and die while doing it.

All in an honest day's work, Chuck thought. He'd be ready for a generous pour of bourbon tonight. Maybe bum one of those cigars from Frank, too. Tim had a bottle of Jack honey in his room, too. A couple of cigars and some good alcohol, a couple of guys sitting around telling lies about the women they'd been with…

Something crashed behind Chuck and he jumped.

When he turned, he saw his other tools had fallen to the ground: his two shovels, extra sledgehammer and his pickaxe. Chuck never used more than that group. Even for a job like this, the biggest he'd ever had to do. Ripping apart a slum tenement in Manhattan was one thing. Tearing down a gutted cement building was another, and he loved the challenge.

He didn't understand why they'd fallen down, though. He always put them in a particular order against the far wall and kept them spread apart so if one fell it wasn't a domino effect.

Yet, it had been, for some reason.

He heard a noise on the stairs leading up to this level.

Chuck waited, expecting someone to come walking up, but the noise stopped.

"Hello? Who's there? Time to break?" Chuck looked out through the gap where the wall used to be and sighed. They were working later than usual, all because they were behind.

Frank had given them the big speech before they'd left the hotel that morning. "The boss has no problem paying overtime. He wants to, in fact, as long as we put in the hours and finish this job. I know we could do it in a fifth of the time with actual equipment, but he wants us to keep our heads down and mouths shut. No one is supposed to know we're here. So far so good."

It wasn't all good, because Chuck could see the fleet of boats hovering all around them. Twice as many as when they'd first started. He was sure several of them were watching them work. He knew it was only a matter of time before they were shut down.

Chuck couldn't care less about the environment, but he cared about doing something illegal and getting tossed in a foreign jail. He didn't speak the language. He didn't understand the currency.

He stood at the edge and relieved himself over the side, laughing to himself. If any of the other guys were anywhere down below, they'd get a surprise everyone would be talking about tonight at dinner. When he was done, he zipped up and gave a salute to the many boats in the water nearby. They were dark shapes now because the sun was dropping quickly over the horizon.

Chuck turned back to the room and frowned. His tools were gone, even the sledgehammer he'd been using a couple of minutes ago.

"Not funny, guys. Give me my stuff back," Chuck said. "The shovel was a present from my mom… her last gift to me before she died in that plane crash in Brazil. Please give it back."

Chuck's mother was alive and well in Matawan, New Jersey, but they didn't know it. They probably knew he was lying, anyway. He made it up as he went along. Part of his charm.

"Seriously, I'm getting angry," Chuck said. "And you don't want to see me when I'm angry." He marched to the stairs, stomping his boots as he moved. Glancing down, all he saw was darkness. "Guess who's not sharing his bourbon tonight? This guy. Buncha jerks."

He went down a flight of stairs, giving up for the day. He'd worked too long and hard anyway. It was time to find Frank, bitch a bit about whoever hid his tools, and get off of this tiny rock.

Chuck stopped when he heard someone walking above him on the floor he'd just been on.

"I don't know how you got behind me, Spiderman, but I'm coming up and there's nowhere for you to go." Chuck stomped back up the stairs, going slow because it was really dark now. Since they'd never worked even close to dusk or night, there'd been no flashlights or lamps to use. The less the mainland saw of them the better, Frank had explained.

When he found out who was messing with him, he was going to one-punch them into oblivion. Chuck made a fist and smiled. He hadn't been in a good fight in far too long. One-punching someone meant only one hit and then they hit the floor. He'd done it only twice in his life, and he'd gotten lucky both times.

This was going to be a great story for tonight, Chuck thought. *I'll leave the jerk up here, too. Let someone else carry him to the boat.*

He stepped back onto the floor and saw his tools were back against the wall. The sky wasn't fully dark yet, a thin orange glow from the sun about to drop over the horizon.

There was no one else on the floor. Unless they'd climbed onto the roof or were dangling off of the side, he was alone.

Chuck went to the side and looked over. He couldn't see anyone. This was getting annoying.

He decided to collect his tools and head to the boat. Whoever it was would get drunk and brag about it, and then Chuck would drop him with a single punch. And take his alcohol for good measure, too.

As he started to collect his tools, he realized his pickaxe was missing.

"This is getting ridiculous," Chuck said and threw up his hands.

A clank behind him spun Chuck around. His pickaxe was dangling at the edge of the open area, barely stuck into the floor.

Chuck got two steps before it fell loose and gravity plummeted it off the side and out of sight.

He cursed and ran to the opening, as if he expected to reach down with fifty-foot arms and catch it before it hit the ground below.

It hit the ground below with a bang, and he knew it had cracked. He'd heard the noise enough to know.

Now he was mad.

Not only was Frank going to get an earful, but everyone who got in his way. Joking around and playing pranks was one thing, but this was just mean. Destroying personal property? The line had been crossed.

Chuck had his tools in hand, wrapping them together and hefting them over his shoulder. He'd need to go slow in the dark.

He got to the next landing down when he heard the noises again from above and sighed.

"I hope you fall off the side in the dark, jerk, and my pickaxe, which you destroyed, jabs you in the family jewels," Chuck yelled.

He turned to keep going and frowned.

Something darker than the darkness moved on the next step, maybe a small animal?

If it was an animal, it had sharp claws. And a bite that ran up his ankle, where the thing sunk its teeth, and shot his leg with so much pain Chuck fell back onto his butt.

Chuck didn't have time to recover or scream because the footsteps that had plagued him from above were joining in, and the feet weren't any of the guys.

They weren't anything human, either. Small. Black.

Chuck saw the teeth and the claws a second before whatever the thing was dropped onto his face and smothered him.

CHAPTER 11

She was in Nagasaki and setting up shop within an hour of Akira's call, since she was already in town. Kris wasn't going to tell him that, of course. Her nagging feeling about where Daisuke was and what had happened to him had kept her awake. After her brief meeting with Akira, she knew she needed boots on the ground.

Or, in her case, a pair of six-inch red heels and a skin-tight matching dress.

Since she wasn't Japanese, she knew she couldn't blend in with the locals. Might as well make an entrance and hope she could garner information from men who'd see her and be weak in the knees. Forget about their drab lives and their boring wives. Eat out of the palm of her hand.

Kris knew she was playing a stereotype and was a disservice to women. She didn't care. They weren't paying her bills. They didn't have to do the things she had to do, so the rest of them could feel good about themselves. She didn't...

She laughed at herself as she fell onto the bed of her hotel room and kicked off her heels, which were killing her feet. She didn't know why she was being dramatic or justifying her actions.

Instead of taking a nap, she changed into her sweatpants and a large t-shirt and pulled out her laptop. She'd need food and a shower but that would be later. Right now, she had work to do.

Daisuke had hired her because he knew what she was really good at and had told her it was a waste to try to work for Akira, since he wouldn't appreciate her skills.

Kris was a hacker. An amateur until she'd been put on the payroll of several of Daisuke's companies. He paid her a small salary, but the bonuses and perks were what got her going: she was paid in cash for the information she extracted from the competition.

The only line she'd draw in the sand was working against Akira, and Daisuke had never asked her to do it. He'd hinted at it, though, and she knew they'd have that argument sooner or later.

If Daisuke is still alive, Kris thought.

Akira had given her the funds to gather information. *Nothing illegal. No bribes. Just intel*, he'd told her.

Kris smiled. He knew how she worked, and what she would or wouldn't do. There wasn't much she wouldn't, which was part of their problem as a couple.

Since she already had access to most of Daisuke's accounts and companies, it was easy to surf through anonymously and see what had changed since the last time she'd been in the system.

Daisuke had tasked her with making sure none of his money or companies were being stripped or money skimmed.

"I'm not paranoid, because it's happening," Daisuke had said and smiled. "Why do you think I got to where I am? By skimming from them myself. By manipulating the funds and the businesses so they look even more attractive. It's all mine. But… if someone else taps into the endless stream of wealth, it can all crash down around me."

Kris knew the worst thing that could happen was someone taking a hard look at his books, and the many deals and gray area moves he'd been making for years.

After a couple of hours with her head down and her nails clicking on the laptop keyboard, she needed a break. She took a quick shower and got dressed conservatively in a simple pair of jeans and a black t-shirt, her hair in a ponytail and tucked under a gray baseball cap. The heels had been swapped out for a pair of black running shoes, and she'd done her makeup as subtle as possible. She wanted to do some recon work tonight.

It had been easy to find out The Texan had hired a small demolition crew out of his home State and brought them to Nagasaki. They had the run of an entire hotel, which The Texan had recently purchased. It meant he had long-term plans for the island.

She walked the few blocks to the hotel and strode inside like she belonged. No use sneaking around. She could play the ditzy blonde if she needed to.

There was no one in the lobby and no one at the front desk.

Wandering the hotel, she found the kitchen. Three men were busy cooking seafood, and it looked and smelled delicious.

At the sight of her, the oldest man, obviously the head chef, frowned at her. He began talking quickly in Japanese.

Kris shook her head and put up her hands. "I'm sorry, I don't understand you, chef. I'm looking for my boyfriend. I wanted to surprise him. He was working on Forbidden Island, he said, whatever that is." She chuckled. "That sounds so mysterious and creepy, right? Any idea if they're back yet?"

"They haven't arrived but they should've been by now," one of the other men said in perfect English. "But you shouldn't be here. No one is supposed to be in the hotel but the staff and the men on the island. You need to leave, ma'am."

Kris nodded. "I'm sorry. I thought it would be fun to surprise him."

The man's eyes narrowed. "What's your boyfriend's name?"

Kris knew he was testing her.

"Frank Meyer. He runs the crew," Kris said. "We haven't dated that long."

The man had a knife in his hand. When Kris stared at it and dramatically swallowed, the man put it on the counter and shrugged. "I doubt that, ma'am. Frank is married. He talks about his wife all the time. Connie."

Kris smiled. "You mean Joy. His wife's name is Joy, and I know all about her. Did he tell you he's going to leave her for me? We're in love."

The chef was yelling in Japanese and waving his hands.

"You must leave. Now."

Kris nodded. "I'm sorry to bother you. When Frank gets back, you'll see it was a misunderstanding. Not a big deal. I'm looking forward to eating this food, too. It smells heavenly."

The man told the chef what she'd said. Kris understood Japanese and a few other languages, which was very useful in her lines of work.

The chef bowed toward her and his face softened a bit.

Kris bowed back and left. No sense in pushing it, and she knew they hadn't arrived back yet. It sounded like they were late, so they might arrive at any minute.

She walked down the street and found a cafe where she could watch the front entrance. As she sat and looked at the menu, it hit her: they were trying to get in and out of Nagasaki without being seen.

Which meant they'd use the most discreet entrance to the hotel, likely an underground parking garage behind the hotel.

Kris shook her head. She was getting slow. It felt good to be out in the real world and doing actual grunt work instead of getting fat sitting on her butt at a computer for hours and working the data.

She ordered a hot tea and *sata andagi*, which was like eating delicious fried dough. The last time she'd had them was in Okinawa, where they'd originated. Kris marveled how, in just a few short years, regional delicacies and dishes had spread across not only Japan but the world. Kris had also ordered *sata andagi*, called simply *andagi*, in Hawaii two years ago.

While on a mini vacation with Akira.

Kris decided to take the direct approach and walk back in through the front door, see if she could find an open room or a janitorial room to sit and wait. While sipping her tea and eating her snack and trying not to think of better days with Akira.

CHAPTER 12

The Texan rubbed his temple with his free hand, his other gripping his phone. He was hoping he'd misheard what Frank had said.

He hadn't. "One of my men is missing. It happened because we stayed an hour and a half later than I wanted to," Frank said.

"It's not about what you want, foreman. It's about what I'm paying you to do. Where could he have gone?" The Texan asked.

"There's only two ways off the island, and he wasn't on the boat," Frank said. "I doubt Chuck hopped over the wall and swam it back."

"You checked the entire island? It's not that big."

Frank groaned on the line. "Of course. A building to building search. We didn't find anything except strange spots that might've been wet."

The Texan sat up. "You found blood?"

"No," Frank said quickly. "But… wet spots on the cement floors, drying. A weird smell, too. Like coppery, still in the air. Marks on the floor through the dust like something heavy had been dragged down the stairs. They stop at the bottom floor and then… nothing."

Coppery might mean blood, but The Texan kept that to himself. This was really bad. Someone getting hurt, falling off of a building was bad enough. That was easily rectified with a payout to the family and a bonus to the men to keep their mouths shut.

A missing man? It meant something odd had happened. It also meant The Texan needed more information before he could proceed.

"Head back to the hotel and await my orders," The Texan said. "Tell the men there will be no work tomorrow, but another search of the island will be in order. Got it?"

Frank paused and The Texan knew what his question was going to be, so he cut the man off. "No authorities. No word of this. You get back and sit tight. Scour the island. It's not that big. If you can't find him… call me. It means he went over the side. Maybe he fell out of a building and no one heard the splash." The Texan tapped his fingers on the desk. "I'll fly Hiro out in the next two days. Give it a thorough search and then back to the hotel. The men will have the rest of tomorrow and the next day off with pay. I don't want anyone in or out of the hotel. Understood, foreman?"

"Yes, sir." Frank cleared his throat. "What if we can't find Chuck?"

"You'll find him," The Texan said. *You have to. There is no other option.* "And when you do, call me directly. Even if Hiro has arrived. I need to be kept in the loop. Got it?"

"There's nowhere for Chuck to go," Frank said quietly, almost to himself. "I saw him go into the building. He was working on it all day. Only took a short break for lunch because he wanted to knock the wall out so he could see the water. When we got up there, he'd done it… but he was gone, and so were his tools. Except for his pickaxe, which we found broken on the ground below."

"Try to be positive. I'm sure he crawled into a hole and took a nap and lost track of time. He'll probably call you tonight and your men can bust his chops about it," The Texan said. "Not a big deal. Trust me. I have a good feeling about it."

When Frank didn't immediately respond, The Texan cleared his throat. "I'll send over some bourbon and beer for your men, too. Let them relax after the search and you find Chick."

"Chuck," Frank said.

"Exactly. It's going to be fine. Keep me updated. Bye." The Texan hung up the phone and sat back in his chair, putting his boots up on the desk and groaning.

This was anything but fine. This was awful.

He had connections in the area, but he didn't know if he could trust any of them.

This would all be much easier if I could find Daisuke alive, or at least a body, The Texan thought. *But I'd rather have him alive.*

The Texan took his boots off the desk and felt it for scratches. He'd been so distracted by the phone call, and the thought of his friend dead.

Daisuke might be a thorn in his side, and they were like water and vinegar when it came to business dealings, but The Texan respected the man. More than anyone he'd ever respected, in fact. From the outset, The Texan knew he'd be a worthy opponent. He was sure Daisuke felt the same way, too. They'd made a lot of money together in a short span of time, but it was always a fact they couldn't work together forever. Both men were Alpha Males. Both wanted all of the money, not a cut of it. Even fifty one percent was too little. One hundred percent or nothing.

I wonder what would've happened if he'd come to me with his plan to reopen the mine and we'd gone in together, The Texan thought. He shook his head. He was missing because he'd jumped into a bad situation and it had nothing to do with The Texan.

He called Hiro and explained the situation.

"I'm leaving in the next hour if possible. How do you want me to handle this?" Hiro asked.

"Quietly. Find a police detective you can trust," The Texan said. *One you can bribe to keep this between them. A cop who won't involve anyone else, and will help to figure this out.*

"I'm on it," Hiro said. He was quiet but didn't hang up.

The Texan smiled. "Say whatever is on your mind, Hiro."

"I was trying to figure out the nicest way to say… when is it time to cut your losses, sir?"

This is why The Texan kept Hiro around. Well, one of the many reasons. The man had guts and said what he was thinking, and if he was asked for his opinion, he never hesitated telling the truth. No matter how negative or bad.

The Texan had subtly leaned on Hiro for a few deals in the past few months, letting him see the bare bone details and seeing if he'd address it. Hiro had every time, and he'd saved the company quite a few dollars.

Eventually The Texan would need to crush him, before he became too smart for his own good, and became a rival.

Like his friend Daisuke.

"There is a line for losses," The Texan finally said. "I haven't crossed it yet, although I can see it a few inches from my cowboy boots."

"And if we cannot find this worker or your former partner and wife?" Hiro asked.

"Then we cut our losses." The Texan stood. "Hit the ground and see what's really happening. If you think they're connected, maybe I rethink this plan. No use throwing bad money after bad money."

"No, sir. I'll call you when I touch down in Japan." Hiro hung up and The Texan began to pace. He felt powerless to do anything, and it was a bad feeling. Even when he was half a world away, he had a good grip on the economics of whatever business was going through something.

This was beyond him, though. Missing people. Sneaking around and skirting the laws and way too much money spent so far without a dime coming back in his direction.

The Texan decided, if this didn't work out completely with Hiro going to figure things out, he was going to pull the plug. Wrap it all up and forget about it.

Forbidden Island could sit and rot for all he cared. There were plenty of other islands in the world to buy and create a paradise. He thought he'd heard the one Johnny Depp owned in the Bahamas was for sale. Maybe the one that the ill-fated Fyre Festival had been on. There were too many possibilities to worry about a sixteen hundred by five hundred piece of cement.

The Texan glanced out his window and saw his family was at the barn again. He'd given his staff explicit instructions not to let the brats on his prized horses again. He knew his family would come to him, whining about it soon enough.

Unless... The Texan decided to fly out to Kimiko Island and take a look for himself.

It was about time he got his hands dirty and his boots wet.

CHAPTER 13

Frank was halfway across his hotel room when he smelled the perfume. He spun around and saw the woman sitting at his desk. She was pretty and she was smiling.

"Don't bother calling out," she said. "I'm only here to talk."

Frank laughed. "Only to talk? I guess my boss didn't send you up to keep me quiet."

"Hardly. The Texan couldn't afford me," she said and winked.

She obviously knew a lot more than he'd thought, especially since not even the men on the crew knew who they were actually working for. Not that most of them would know who he was, anyway.

Frank wondered whether he could make a break for the door or simply grab her and slam her to the floor. Was she a thief? She was an American, so obviously not a local. Had one of the boys put her up to this? Trying to mess with the only married guy on the crew, and their boss?

"I think it's time for you to leave, miss, whoever you are and whoever sent you," Frank said. He put his hand out and motioned for her to get up.

She didn't budge. Despite being dressed down, she was attractive. *And I'm a married man who loves my wife*, Frank reminded himself. No matter what she thought was going to happen or had been paid to do by his jerk of a crew, it wasn't going to.

"Let me guess... you're a cop. FBI. CIA. Something with initials. Maybe one of the guys owes child support," Frank said.

She laughed. "Oh, I can guarantee at least one of these guys owes a woman money for a kid, but that's not why I'm here."

Frank swept his hand from her to the door. "I asked you to leave."

"Men never ask me to leave their hotel room." She grinned. "That's not why I'm here, though, Frank. I need your help."

"Here we go," he said and groaned. "I'm a foreman on a job. Nothing more to it than that. I think you've got the wrong guy. I've seen enough movies to know an American on foreign soil getting involved with a mysterious and pretty woman often ends up with him as the patsy and in prison, while you walk away with a truckload of gold bars or something."

"You think I'm mysterious and pretty? You should see me when I'm all dressed up. I turn heads," she said. "Have a seat. I only want to talk. If I was an assassin I would've shot you as soon as you entered the room, two shots to the head with a silencer so no one heard it. Then I'd put on sunglasses as the perfect disguise and leave the hotel, never to be seen again."

"If you're not a deadly assassin sent to kill me by an ex-girlfriend from high school… who are you?"

She lowered her hand and Frank sat on the edge of the bed, ready to spring if he needed to. He was off his game today, especially since they hadn't found Chuck. He knew the right thing to do was to call the police, but he knew he'd be fired. He hoped Hiro coming would sort it all out. By then maybe Chuck would reappear and they could have a drink and laugh about it.

But Frank doubted that was going to happen. This might've been his last day on the job before it was shut down… and now this woman was confusing him.

"My name is Kris Scarlet."

Frank laughed. "Sounds like a stripper name."

"I went by K.C. Sass when I worked in Las Vegas," she said. "There were already too many Cinnamons and Delilahs working before I got there."

"That's a wonderful story." Frank spread his hands. "Now tell me why you're here, in my room."

"I need information about Forbidden Island."

Frank smiled. "The boss calls it Kimiko Island. Has a better ring to it. Not that I care. Just doing my job."

"I'm going to need to be kept in the loop about whatever is happening on the island," Kris said. "No matter how big or small."

Frank stood. "Well, that isn't going to happen, so it's time for you to leave."

She surprised him by standing, too. She was much shorter than he'd thought, but she seemed tough to him. "What can I do to get you on my team?"

Frank shook his head. "Nothing. I'm perfectly happy doing what I'm doing, and not doing anything I will regret. Besides, I don't know anything other than the job. You're barking up the wrong tree."

Kris shook her head. "I'm not going to waste my time or yours with idle threats, or any of that mess. I'll pay you. Handsomely. All I need is information about what's happening, since I can't go onto the island."

"We're demoing the island. That's it. Nothing more than that," Frank said.

Kris cocked her head. "Then why did it take you so long to return today? Every other day you've been back in the hotel before dark. Well before, in fact."

Frank looked away. She'd been watching them. For how long? What did she really want? He'd had enough. "I'm going to call the police. This conversation is done." He turned to reach for the phone in the room and realized there wasn't one. He fished his cell phone from his pocket.

Kris grabbed his face and kissed him.

A long, passionate kiss, and he didn't immediately push her away. When he did, he wiped his mouth with the back of his hand. "What are you doing?"

She took a step back. He saw she had her phone in hand and was typing furiously.

"You took a picture?" Frank asked.

She shook her head and put her phone into her waistband. He noticed she wasn't wearing underwear and felt guilty. "I shot a video of us making out. Then I sent it to a couple of my hidden email accounts, so even if you decided to do something really stupid like take my phone and break it, too bad. Would it surprise you to know I did some research about you, Frank Meyer?"

She started rattling off about where he lived, where he went to school, the jobs he'd worked and his wife's name. Where she worked. What her phone number was.

Frank sat down on the bed and put his hands on his face. He groaned. "Why are you doing this to me? I'm a good man. A hard worker. I don't deserve this."

"I feel bad," Kris said. He knew that was a lie.

"Then erase the video." Frank wondered if it was really all that bad. He could call his wife and explain to her what had happened. She'd believe him. Right?

Kris smiled. "I'm an expert at manipulating video, too. It would be easy to film me having sex with someone about your build and putting your head on his instead. Grainy footage so your wife couldn't see your birthmarks and your junk. There's only one way to get this to go away."

Frank shook his head.

"Think about it. I'll call you with my number. If you want to work with me, I promise you the video will be destroyed," Kris said. "I have nothing against you, Frank. This isn't personal. You seem like a great guy, and your wife is lovely. I promise you. This isn't anything illegal. I'm not asking you to steal documents or kill someone. All I need is a daily phone call with everything strange or pertinent that happened. Not so hard. No lies, either. No hiding things or I'll have to do what I have to do." She walked to the door but didn't leave. "Starting with today. Why did you get back so late? What happened?"

Frank sighed and told her about Chuck missing.

CHAPTER 14

Tim Buda was tired of this. *Damn Chuck playing games again, or maybe he's in a brothel with a couple of hot women while we're wasting time looking for him.*

The island was small. They'd gone over it three times already, sweeping in and out of each building. He never thought he'd say it, but he wanted to get back to work. Breaking rocks and tossing them into the barge. It was better than this.

Frank gathered them near the gate, the boat a few feet away in the water.

"Time to quit this mess and go home?" Tim asked. "Or can we get back to work?"

Frank frowned. "One of our own is missing. I guess that doesn't mean anything to you?"

"Of course it does, Frank… but you know as well as I do what Chuck is capable of. Remember the time in El Paso when he disappeared for two days?"

A couple of the men who'd been on the crew with them nodded.

"This isn't El Paso," Frank said. He smiled. "And that was extenuating circumstances. They were triplets and he apologized. He couldn't do much work afterward, of course."

"Or walk straight for a couple of days," Tim said. He tried to laugh and failed. He knew this wasn't Chuck catching a lucky break with some local women and forgetting about the job, especially since Tim had been the one in El Paso that had told Chuck they were going to be off an extra two days because of some Texan or Mexican holiday. Chuck had never ratted out his buddy, taking the hit.

Tim felt bad he'd been so selfish now, thinking only of himself. "I'll keep looking, if that's alright with you, Boss Man."

Frank hated when they called him that, but he simply nodded. "Everyone else get back to work. Now we're even more behind and we'll be working late again."

As everyone groaned, Tim walked off. He'd start where they'd last seen Chuck and work his way up and down the collapsing steps, dodging falling masonry and bird poop.

"Chuck, where are you buddy? I got a bottle of Calumet in my hotel room. I don't mind sharing, even though you'd never share a sip of your precious Woodford Reserve." Tim stared at the wall he'd destroyed and shook his head. The man did excellent work. He'd taken out an entire wall without losing the structural integrity of the building. Like it was nothing.

The water between the island and the mainland was jammed with fishing boats, all getting too close for comfort. He knew there were probably a few cameras trained on him and the others, especially when they were higher than the walls and working in the buildings.

Tim backed away and did another sweep of the floors. It was eerie to be here, and while some of the guys got used to what they found, he hadn't yet.

Toys littered the floor of one room, broken and filthy. Mold still grew on the plates and silverware on a kitchen table, the legs rotting. It would collapse soon enough. Without glass in any of the windows, the animals had made nests and there were desiccated droppings on most surfaces.

In a closet, Tim found a pile of bird bones. What had done that? It might be fifty different birds that had been picked clean. The door was closed. Had it been before they'd been searching for Chuck? Maybe one of the others wasn't as easy with this place as they were letting on.

Four buildings later and still no sign of Chuck. The people who'd left the island had done so quickly. Tim had done some research when they'd first arrived, figuring there were ghosts of thousands who'd been tortured and killed on this rock. While it had been a prison during the war, and the prisoners had been forced to mine the coal, over a thousand of them had died. Those who hadn't still lived in squalor, in these seven floor concrete buildings.

What blew Tim's mind was the thought of people coming to live and work here after the war. Over five thousand people on this small island, piled on top of one another. Families in one room while the husband went down below to extract the coal. This must've been an awful place to live.

Tim wondered about it being abandoned so suddenly again. According to official documents he'd found online, it was simply that the coal was no longer needed because Japan had switched fully into petroleum. That answer made sense, until you were walking in the footsteps of someone from over forty years ago and saw what they'd left behind.

As Tim got closer to the area where the mine entrance was, he saw three large rats scurrying from a crack in the wall. He realized he'd seen plenty of bones but this was the first actual living creature he'd seen. Birds circled but rarely landed, and if they did they were easily spooked back into the air.

Had the crew scared the creatures into the underground, or were there only a small number left? Tim imagined the birds feasting on the rats, swooping down and snatching them. Death from above.

The crack wasn't big enough for much more than the rats, but Tim took his flashlight off of his belt and shined the light inside.

Tim jumped back because he thought he heard a growl and something scuffling on the other side.

"Hey… who's in there?" Tim felt like an idiot. It was a rat or some predator that liked to eat rats. He doubted it was going to answer him.

And then it did, a whimper. Like someone in pain. It even spoke, although Tim had no idea what it had said. It sounded like a little girl, in fact. Deep within the tunnel, the sound echoing.

There was someone inside.

Tim yanked at the thick metal door that had been erected in front of the mine entrance, expecting it to hold tight and not give. He frowned when it came loose easily, sliding across the ground like it had been well-oiled and had been used every day like it was nothing.

He peered inside, shining the light. "Hello?" Tim didn't know how to say hello in Japanese. He'd brought an English to Japanese dictionary with him, the idea to go old school and learn some basic words, but the book was still on his nightstand in the hotel untouched.

Looking around, he saw he'd opened the side door. He imagined this was where the prisoners and later the workers had entered the shaft, the larger door for the supplies. The tracks were still visible in the dirt and he could smell the musty air mixed with coal dust. It was stifling.

"I'm going to get you help," Tim said.

His answer was another cry of pain and a few more words. They sounded more urgent.

"Chuck? Is that you?" Tim knew it didn't sound like his buddy. But who else could it be?

Every impulse told Tim to turn and run. Get help. They could get a few men inside and scout around. Do a proper search. He'd assumed the mine was off limits, but they needed to find Chuck. And save whoever was down here, too.

Tim scanned with his flashlight again but didn't see anyone. He took a couple of steps forward. There was something just out of his range. He could see the hint of someone small. Was it really a child down in the mine? That didn't make any sense.

"Hello?" Tim took a few more steps but could feel the walls closing in on him the further he got from the entrance. He turned back to make sure the door was still open and frowned. It was closing, and someone small was near it.

When the figure turned and Tim shone his light in its red eyes, it cried out and tried to flee.

Tim didn't know what kind of animal it was. It stood on two legs, was about three feet tall and covered in either coal dust or thick short black hair.

He tried to follow it with the light, but the thing was quick and leapt onto the wall. Tim noticed the sharp claws digging into the rock as it was up and onto the roof of the tunnel.

Tim turned and shone the light. He blinked.

There were now two of them, overhead.

He heard something approaching.

Another three were charging at him. Tim turned to flee and felt the claws digging into his back and legs. They were sharper than he thought, his last thought before one leapt from the ceiling and stomped on his flashlight.

Plunging him into darkness. Before he could call out, they began to feast.

CHAPTER 15

The Texan had just pulled up to his private jet when his phone rang. He didn't recognize the number. "Yeah?"

"Is this Rutger Paisley?"

"Whatever you're selling, buddy, I'm not buying. Lose my number," The Texan said. He pulled the phone away from his ear and was about to stab at the disconnect button.

"I have a video of your missing worker," the voice yelled. "Don't hang up. Hear me out."

The Texan stared at the phone for a second before putting it on speakerphone and onto the desk. "Talk. You have one minute."

"I work for... well, that's not important," the man on the other end said.

The Texan didn't recognize the voice but he'd already hit the record button on his desk phone. He'd have the conversation to analyze later, and if this idiot tried to bribe him or say anything illegal, he'd have him.

"I've been filming your men on Forbidden Island for weeks."

The Texan smiled. He knew they were being watched. No big deal. They weren't doing anything illegal. He owned the island. "It's been renamed to Kimiko Island... who am I speaking to?"

"That's not important," the man said quickly.

"Oh, but it is to me." The Texan wrote down the phone number the man was calling from and took out one of his other cell phones from his desk, messaging Hiro the number and wanting to know who it was, why they had his private number and why they might have potentially damaging video.

"Your man was working on the top floor of a building," the man said. "He, uh... was attacked?" He said it as if it were a question. "It was too dark to get perfect footage, but I've had one of the guys in the newsroom back home analyze it."

"And where is back home? Los Angeles? New York? Cedar Rapids?" The Texan knew this stranger had a New York exchange. He might be working for one of the big networks. Maybe a cable channel. Heck, he could be a reporter for TMZ. If he was a freelance, he might be asking for a payout from The Texan to squash it before he went to the networks with the footage. If there really was any footage.

"Again... not important. What is important is that I have the footage."

"Then send it to me," The Texan said.

"Not until we come up with, uh, a deal."

The Texan laughed. "Let me get this straight: you say you have a video of one of my men who is missing on Kimiko Island... except none of my men are missing. In fact, I just spoke to my foreman and I think he would've told me. You're barking up the wrong tree. Unless you can prove to me what you say is true… I'm hanging up."

He knew the man wasn't bluffing and had video of the guy who was missing. The Texan couldn't remember his name, but a video might show what happened to him. Of course, if it was foul play or an accident or whatever it was, he'd need to proceed with caution.

"I'll email you a clip of it," the man said. "I want a hundred thousand dollars for the full video."

"Ridiculous," The Texan said. "How do I know you won't try to sell it even if I pay you? Not that I will. Bribery is a serious offense, and I have friends in very high places." The Texan smiled when Hiro texted back the information. "Now… let me see it."

"But… you just said you weren't going to meet my demands."

The Texan sighed. "Maybe I'm feeling generous today. Maybe I'll surprise you and give in to your demands. Of course, I still think you're lying. And I still don't see a video."

Hiro messaged The Texan, making him smile. The man was worth his salary and so much more.

"Just a few seconds," the man said. "Sending it now. I'll call back with my updated demands in two minutes. I need your email."

The Texan gave him one of the emails Hiro had set up for just such an occasion. He was glad he'd still had it written on a sheet in his desk.

"Two minutes," the man said, sounding more confident now.

The Texan didn't say anything, waiting for the file. After a couple of silent minutes, the man hung up.

When he saw the file appear in his email, he texted Hiro.

Two minutes later, the man tried to call back but The Texan ignored it. Hiro was calling at the same time.

"What do we have?"

"It looks legitimate, and it is distressing," Hiro said. "I was able to follow it back to this idiot's computer and download it completely. Then I erased it from his hard drive and emails. It looks like he sent it to a few people. If they haven't opened it, when they do their system will crash and wipe out everything. The two I saw that had opened it are being infected as we speak."

"Let me see it." The Texan sat back and stared at his phone.

The video was dark and grainy and from a distance. The camera, shaky because it was filmed while on water, showed a man peeing off the side of the hole in the building.

Something small and dark moved behind him.

The man turned back and The Texan held the phone close to his face, trying to decipher what he was seeing.

"I'm having a man fix the video, but I'm pretty sure some small wild animals are on the island. They clearly attacked him, and they might be responsible for the disappearance of Daisuke and Kimiko, too." Hiro sighed. "What do you need me to do? I'll be in Nagasaki soon. Pull the men?"

"Yes. Shut it down. I'll call the foreman and have them go back to the hotel. Meet them there and see if they've seen anything." The Texan smiled. "Thanks for such a great job."

The phone was ringing again, the man trying to reach The Texan.

"I'll call when I get the information," Hiro said.

The Texan hung up on Hiro and answered the other call.

"Why didn't you answer? I told you what would happen," the man said.

"I saw the footage. Feel free to send it to everyone." The Texan laughed. "I dare you."

"Fine. I gave you a chance, Paisley."

"And I look forward to seeing what your next move is going to be once you figure it out... John W. Smith." The Texan laughed again. "Even your name is boring."

"How did you... it doesn't matter."

The Texan put his boots on the desk and smiled, waiting for Smith to figure it out.

The groan came a few seconds later. "What did you do?"

"I took care of it myself," The Texan said. "And as soon as I get off the phone with you, I'm going to call your boss and his boss. All the way to the top. Your career, as small as it was, is now over. You'll never get another job in the media business. You know why? Because I control it, you moron."

"No. I sent it to others…"

"They're going to be so mad at you when they open the file to discover their computer is now a very large paperweight," The Texan said. "You tried to play with the big dogs and you lost, Smith. Good luck trying to find a job as a janitor now. Have a nice day."

The Texan laughed and disconnected the call.

He decided to pour himself a nice glass of scotch before beginning his calls to ruin Smith's life. The Texan so enjoyed having a mission, even if it only lasted a few conversations.

CHAPTER 16

The body was rotting somewhere nearby. Kimiko could smell the blood and it made her sick. She'd gagged and dry-heaved a few times already. The air was so stale and without any breeze, the smell of death clung to her.

Kimiko sat up when she heard something large being dragged and getting closer.

The creatures dropped it off at the entrance to her room. She counted to ten silently, wondering if they'd enter or retreat.

When she heard them fading away, she gave it another ten count before standing and walking slowly across to where it had been dropped, whatever it was.

Kimiko felt around on the ground and found a body. She recoiled and looked around, even though she couldn't see anything. Was this the same rotting corpse she'd been smelling for hours? The stench wasn't stronger. How many more people had been killed?

She knelt down on the ground and tried to keep calm, the thought this was Daisuke overwhelming. She took a deep breath and felt around, touching the face first.

It was not her husband. This man had some stubble, he was skinnier and had higher cheekbones than Daisuke. He also had long hair. She'd thought it was a woman at first until she felt down the body and touched his man parts, pulling her hand back and feeling embarrassed.

Kimiko listened for movement in the dark. Was she being watched? It seemed likely.

She put her head down on the man's chest, wondering who he was. The smell of his cooling blood and his innards made her gag. She fought the urge to get away, knowing what she had to do. Hoping the creatures were still outside the room and couldn't see what she was doing, she acted like she was sobbing as she moved a hand into the man's pockets.

His wallet was useless. Kimiko turned the body, giving an exaggerated howl, and searched his other front pocket. When her fingers touched a hard object, she slipped it out and put it in her pocket. She knew it was a lighter.

The man had a tool belt on as well, but whatever he'd been carrying on it was gone. She tried to unhook the tool belt but she heard something shuffling toward her and stopped.

She knew the creatures were close. She could smell them. There might be a few of them.

Kimiko crawled a few feet back. They grabbed the body and began dragging it away.

Why had they left it for her, for a few minutes? Was it a warning?

"Where is my husband?" Kimiko asked.

The dragging noises stopped. She thought she heard a grunt further down the tunnel.

Kimiko put her back to the wall. It was the only way she'd know they were not behind her. The only thing she had left.

The grunting was closer, and it was being answered.

Kimiko braced herself and could smell the creatures as they closed in on her.

She decided, if this was her last stand, she'd need to be defiant. Stand her ground in the darkness. Die an honorable death. But first…

"Where is my husband?" Kimiko asked again, chin up and staring at where she hoped they were standing.

She heard a deep growl but didn't squirm. Tried not to show fear, even though she felt like throwing up and crying.

The grunts had ceased.

She felt the presence of one of them, probably the leader, inches from her face. Could smell his must. Could imagine his nostrils flaring as he sniffed her. Was he trying to smell her fear?

Kimiko opened her mouth but a thick hand covered her face and pushed her back roughly against the wall.

Kuu, the monster said. It grunted and she could hear the smile on its lips as it released her and turned to leave.

She knew they were all walking away, and she could do nothing but slide to the floor and begin to cry.

Kuu. Eat.

Daisuke had been eaten by these creatures.

She felt like she had nothing left to live for.

Kimiko clutched the lighter in her hand and wondered if it would make sense to end it now. Set fire to her dirty clothing and hope she died before they could put it out.

CHAPTER 17

Hiro wasn't surprised to see a pretty woman in the hotel, but he was surprised who it was.

"Miss Scarlet… what are you doing here?" Hiro asked, sitting in the chair next to her in the lobby. It was dark outside and he was tired, hoping to talk to the crew before they were too drunk or passed out to understand what he was saying or asking.

She smiled. "I am at a disadvantage. You know me but I don't know you."

Hiro laughed. "Oh, I have no doubt you know who I am, where I went to school and what my favorite food is."

"You seem fond of ribeye and a cold beer in your leisure time, as short as it is."

Hiro knew he'd need to play this correctly. Kris Scarlet was going to be a tough nut to crack, as the saying went. She was here for Akira. Hiro wished he was seated across from Akira, because the man could be manipulated. He knew from research Kris wasn't going to budge on anything she set her mind to. Now he needed to figure out what she had set her mind on.

"I also prefer a good scotch," Hiro said. He grinned. "Tell me, Miss Scarlet…"

She waved her hand. "Please, Hiro, call me Kris. I insist."

Hiro shrugged. "If you insist, Kris. As I was saying," he turned in his chair so he had an eye on the front doors and her. It wasn't that he didn't trust her, which he supposed he'd be insane to do, but because he knew she was waiting for the men from the island. Which meant they hadn't returned yet, which was troubling. He decided beating around the bush with her wasn't going to get him anywhere. "I'm guessing I haven't arrived too late to see the crew back safe and sound."

Kris glanced at the door before locking her pretty eyes back on Hiro. "Buy me a drink, sailor."

Hiro stood and offered his hand, which she took and rose from the chair.

"Such a gentleman," she said and turned, giving him a nice view of her backside, framed in a red dress.

Keep focused. She is here to distract and manipulate, Hiro thought. *She's also on a fact-finding mission, the same as I am*.

He followed her to the bar, keeping his eyes on the back of her head in case she turned and caught him in a weak position.

"Two scotches," Kris said to no one, since there was no bartender.

Hiro laughed. "We didn't think it prudent to pay someone to run around and fix drinks to a dozen rowdy workers each night. We were sure whoever we hired would quit, too. These men can drink, as the bill for whiskey each week rivals most other expenses."

Kris walked around to the other side of the bar and found a bottle of scotch hidden underneath. She poured two glasses, took a sip and slid his across the bar.

Hiro pointed behind her. "All of the bottles have been emptied and refilled with water. They look nice from the lobby, but once you get this close you can see what happened."

Kris reached back and took down a bottle. Some of the water was missing. "I wonder how many were sampled until they realized it."

Hiro swept his hand. "It looks like most." He had to laugh. "I made sure the men understood to pace themselves with the supplies each week." He put his head down and lifted his glass. "Of course, by day four they're asking for more."

"They're bored. They can't leave the hotel or mingle with the locals. They rise early, get on a boat for the island, and usually arrive before dark. That's a lot of hours to kill with TV they can't understand, playing cards and drinking," Kris said. "It's a wonder they aren't asking for more every two days."

"This is true." Hiro lifted his glass to eye level. "Here's a toast to us... whatever this actually is, Miss Scarlet."

"Two people who understand what's really going on, sir." She clinked her glass against his and took a sip of the scotch. "Now... where is Daisuke and his wife?"

Hiro chuckled. "Do you honestly think I know what happened to them? I don't, and neither does The Texan. Yes, you know he took advantage of their disappearance and took control of many assets still in his name. But wouldn't you do the same thing if you had the chance?"

Kris smiled. "Of course. Without a thought, even if it was my partner."

"Former partner," Hiro corrected.

"Legally still partners in many instances, or The Texan wouldn't have the island right now." Kris took another sip. "It's in poor taste, don't you think? The couple haven't been missing for that long. Presumed dead, of course, but not in any legal dcfinition. If they suddenly appeared, what would happen to the plans put into motion?"

Hiro stared into his glass. She was cunning. Came at you when you had your guard down. A fine foe indeed. "What would you do in this exact situation?"

Kris put her glass on the bar. "We'd both do the same exact thing. Obviously. It looks tacky, though, you have to admit. A public relation nightmare if Daisuke and Kimiko arc alive. Especially if they're being held somewhere against their will. That might even finally sink The Texan. No amount of his money would clear his already soiled name from such an embarrassment."

"I hope you're not implying my boss is dirty," Hiro said. He was staring at Kris now. He needed to maintain eye contact. Let her know he wasn't going to be rattled by her words and accusations again. "Especially working for Daisuke."

Kris pushed the glass away. "No one is free from ego and greed."

"What about your former beau, Akira?" Hiro hid his smile but he was sure Kris hadn't been expecting that comment.

She grinned. "It looks like you did your homework on me, sir. Not many know that fact or think it important."

"All facts are important in our business."

"And what business is that? I wonder sometimes," Kris said. Her cell phone buzzed in her small purse and she shrugged. "Sorry to cut this fascinating back and forth short, but I'm sure it's an important call."

Hiro bowed his head. "I'm sure. Will I be seeing you again, ma'am? Can I offer you a room somewhere in town?"

Kris took out her phone and began walking toward the elevator. "Thank you, but I'll be staying here. One of your strong workers has taken a shine to me."

Hiro kept his smile until she entered the elevator and it closed.

He watched to make sure it was moving before calling The Texan.

"Kris Scarlet is in town. In the hotel, in fact. I just had a drink with her. She's gotten her hooks in one of the men. She knows too much," Hiro said. "Speaking of the workers… they haven't returned yet."

The Texan groaned. "Call Frank. See what's happening. Do I need to get on a plane and fly out there, or can you handle this?"

Hiro knew, if The Texan had to get on a plane and fly out, he'd be looking for a new job. "I have this under control. I wanted to call you first since we had two different problems at once. I'll keep you up to date."

He hung up before The Texan could take out his frustrations on Hiro.

Frank's number went to voicemail.

Hiro finished his scotch and then hers as well.

CHAPTER 18

Tim was now missing, too. Frank had wasted an hour looking for him, the men doing another sweep of the island and finding nothing.

Where had two of his men gone?

"I think we cut our losses and go back to the hotel," Frank said. He'd made sure they were paired up in twos as they searched and were within sight of at least one other group at all times.

The men, tired and scared, followed Frank to the gate.

He'd need to call The Texan as soon as they arrived safely and explain the situation. He knew without anyone saying what the crew was thinking: there was no amount of money to stay another minute on this island.

Frank didn't blame them, either. He knew he was going to have a long night trying to explain to The Texan why his men were packing up and going home. He could see it in their eyes. They were scared, and he knew his face betrayed the same emotion.

He'd have to contend with the woman back at the hotel, too. Frank had told her too much already, and he knew she wasn't finished getting what she wanted from him. He'd told her about the crew, what they were doing, the locals being paid off or clueless, and the orders The Texan was feeding him. He knew she'd feed it back to whoever was interested. Information was not a two-way street with Kris Scarlet.

"This is overtime," one of the men said. "I expect to get paid for it, but I'll be damned if I step foot on this rock again."

A few of the men were agreeing, and Frank put his hands up. His flashlight was on, and it cut a beam into the darkness. "I get it. I'll talk to the boss and see what he says."

"I spoke my piece. I don't care what he says."

Frank nodded. He didn't want to waste more time and spend another minute on this island. They'd figure it out in the hotel. "Let's get out of here already."

Chuck and Tim would be found. He knew it. They were safe. Maybe they'd somehow gotten off the island and were halfway back to Texas. He knew they hadn't dived into the sea, though. The sharks were always nearby, and a few of the men had tossed the rest of their lunch into the water like idiots. Feeding sharks wasn't a smart thing, because it brought even more of them.

Frank threw open the gate and frowned.

The boat was missing.

He stepped onto the small landing and looked down into the water and saw it with his flashlight, the boat on its side and sunken. A large gash on the side.

"What is it?" The men behind him were trying to see what Frank was seeing.

Frank turned and waved his hands. "Everyone back up, please and thank you. We have a situation." *It's more than a situation*, he thought. *This is going to create chaos and panic throughout the men.*

He could feel it rising in himself.

"Where's the boat?"

Frank closed the gate and looked past the men, looking for somewhere they could be safe. Safe from what, though? He knew the boat had been sunk by something. Sharks didn't do that. They didn't rip apart a ship. Where was the captain? No one had heard a scream.

"We need to conserve our lights," Frank said. "Let's head to the nearest building and set up a perimeter."

"For what?"

Frank didn't answer the man, walking with purpose. He needed to keep it together.

His phone rang and he answered it, trying to walk away from prying ears, but his men were a step behind. Again, he couldn't blame them.

"How's it going over there?" It was Kris, sounding sweet. Unsettlingly sweet. "I thought you'd be back by now, and we could have another chat."

Frank closed his eyes. "I told you already… leave me alone. Get out of my room and the hotel. Stop. I'm a happily married man and I like my job."

"Who are you talking to?" one of the men asked.

"Did I give you the wrong signals, Frank? I'm sorry. I never came on to you. If I had... you'd be wondering what happened, if you should confess to your wife, and why can't sex be as great with her as it is with me." Kris laughed. "Hiro is here. I imagine your boss is also coming, too. Things are beyond either of our control, Frank. I'm just wondering how I can help you."

You can help by getting us off this island, Frank thought. "Is Hiro with you?"

"Not at the moment. I left him, confused, in the bar. He's curious why I'm here and who I've been shacking up with."

Frank groaned. He didn't want to lose his job, and he knew she'd already alerted Hiro that he'd said too much.

"Now, now... even if they're stupid enough to fire you because of me, rest assured, Akira will hire you. I'll make sure of it. I have a lot of pull with him, you know?"

"I need to call Hiro," Frank said. He disconnected and called Hiro.

"Where are you?" Hiro asked, anger in his voice.

"The boat sank," Frank said and shook his head. He was glad to see the men had walked into the nearest building and he could see they'd started a small fire. "No, the boat was somehow damaged and went down. I have no clue where the captain is, or Chuck and Tim."

"You now have two men missing, and the captain?"

"Yes. Send another boat. We need to get off this island. If we spend a night here... I think a few guys are going to lose it. Hurry. We're near the gate. Call me when you're close," Frank said.

Hiro was silent for a minute. "Who do you think it is?"

"I have no idea. There isn't anywhere for someone to hide. Maybe an animal? Not sure where it would hide, either." Frank looked down the street into the darkness. "The only place we haven't searched is the mine tunnel."

"You boarded it up. No?"

"It's the only place," Frank said. "Get us off this rock. We're done. Let The Texan know no amount of money will bring the men back, but I'll do it as long as we are armed and have enough manpower to go into the tunnel. We might find our men. We might find whatever is doing this."

"I will make arrangements and call The Texan immediately. Hang tight. I'll be on the boat, too," Hiro said.

Frank went inside the building and all eyes turned toward him.

"We'll set a two-man watch outside and two inside," Frank said. "I don't imagine we'll be here for more than an hour. They're sending a new boat to pick us up." He put his hand in the air when a few mouths looked like they were going to start yapping. "I've already let management know we're done. Not coming back to this island. I already have another offer for us, so we're good. I've had enough of Japan for a while."

It worked, because no one commented. They spread out and talked in twos and threes, whispering, as if whatever evil had befallen their crew members and the captain of the boat might be listening.

Frank felt a definite chill even though the air was hot, even though it had been dark for hours.

Two men went outside. Another two headed toward the other end of the floor, near gaps where the windows had been.

Frank settled down, his back to the wall, and made sure his phone was in hand so he wouldn't miss the call.

A few minutes later, the first scream broke the silence.

CHAPTER 19

"They never came back," Kris said as soon as Akira answered. "Neither did the boat or the captain. Again. It happened again."

"Who is there with you?"

"Hiro, The Texan's right-hand man. I have him under control," Kris said. "He's still sleeping. I had to step out into the hall to talk."

Akira closed his eyes and bit his lip. He was jealous. Mad because she was with another man, even though they'd been broken up for awhile. He had the sneaking suspicion she'd slept with his father, too, but couldn't prove it. She'd never tell. If he came right out and asked if she'd slept with Hiro, she'd deflect and have a laugh at his expense. Kris only ever gave you the small piece of information she wanted you to have, and it was usually so small it gave you more questions than answers.

"I'm coming," Akira said. "Stay where you are and keep monitoring the situation."

"It will take you hours to get here," Kris said.

Akira smiled. "I'm already in Japan. Eddie and I cleared my schedule. I had a bad feeling something was going to happen."

"You didn't trust me to do what needed to be done?"

Akira shook his head, even though she couldn't see it. "I knew you'd keep it under control. Do what you have to do." *Like sleep with the enemy.*

Kris didn't say anything, and Akira thought they'd been disconnected.

"Are you still there?" Akira asked.

"He's on the move. I think the men on the island are in trouble. I tried calling Frank back but he didn't answer," Kris said. "Hiro is leaving the hotel. I'm going to follow."

"Keep me in the loop." Akira went to Eddie's room and knocked.

Eddie answered with suitcases packed and fully dressed. "Are we ready to go to Nagasaki?"

"As quickly as possible. Men are missing. I've started research on the island itself, and there are some dark things I've found," Akira said. "Not just the official documents, either. There were attacks and disappearances during World War II, and several children went missing in 1974. Right before they abandoned Forbidden Island for good."

"I found a website filled with Bigfoot and Chupacabra sightings. Tales of kaiju and sea monsters. Aliens taking the form of humans. That kind of nonsense. But I did find supposed interviews with a child who left the island with his family, and he has a story no one believed. No one wanted to, anyway. I'll show you on the plane," Eddie said.

Akira took a deep breath. "How long would it take to hire an army of men?"

Eddie frowned. "How many?"

"I want to bring with us at least two dozen, well-armed and ready for whatever happens." Akira's mind was going a mile a minute. "See if you can find explosive devices and the people to use them."

"Dynamite? Really?"

Akira nodded. "Pay them double what they're worth. I need them to be ready when we land."

"It will take too long to go through the proper channels and get explosives," Eddie said.

Akira knew what he was going to say would stun Eddie, but he felt like they were on the clock now. The longer Forbidden Island was above water the longer it was a danger. "Don't go through the proper channels, then. I want men who don't necessarily work for a corporation or can be traced back to me. Do you understand?"

Eddie nodded his head slowly. "Are you sure about this?"

"It's the only way." Akira put his head down. "I'm cutting corners like my father. I get it. But... I need to do this. If we get bogged down in red tape, this could drag on for years. In the end, I don't have a claim on the island. My father will be declared dead, and The Texan will build his resort or whatever else he wants. More and more people will die, and he'll pay off whoever he needs to in order to keep it going. He only cares about the money."

"Once you cross this line…" Eddie stared at Akira, who didn't blink.

"I'll have a plane ready by the time we get to the airport, and I'll start making calls. I might know a guy." Eddie smiled. "I never thought I'd need to make a call like this, but it's always good to have these types in your connections just in case."

"Hopefully I'll never have to do this again," Akira said.

They were in the air within the hour and Eddie had procured the proper teams, but Akira didn't want to know the specifics. He would never let Eddie take the fall in the event this all went south, but right now he was only worried about his parents… and Kris.

He knew she was going to be in the middle of this. No way the woman stayed in the hotel and watched from the sidelines. Kris Scarlet was going to be wherever Hiro was, wherever the action was.

Akira hoped he wasn't going to arrive too late.

He checked his messages several times, but there was no word from Kris. He tried calling her twice, but she didn't answer. Was she too busy gathering information, or was it something else?

Eddie was busy moving money into offshore accounts and doing things Akira swore he'd never ask his friend to do. They'd been through a lot together, and he knew Eddie was disappointed. He'd help and they'd do what needed to be done, but Akira felt like the relationship would be damaged. Irreparably.

Would Eddie quit or need a break? Akira would let him do whatever needed to be done. Their friendship was more important than anything else.

Eddie looked up from his laptop and gave Akira a smile. "We should arrive shortly. I have cars and two boats on standby. If we're lucky, the government won't know we're even there. I won't tell you the amount of money you had to shell out for this."

Akira shook his head. "I don't want to know."

He stared out the window at the clouds. He never wanted to know the cost of selling off part of his soul, even if it might get his parents back.

CHAPTER 20

The two men stationed outside the building were missing.

Frank called out for both men, but all he heard was the wind in return. Where was Hiro? He prayed the man wasn't taking his sweet time rescuing them.

The rest of the men were bunched together in the doorway now.

Frank wanted to say something to calm them down, but his hands were shaking.

A faint scraping noise from above their heads on the uppermost floors had them all looking up at the same time.

"Someone is up there," someone said. Frank didn't know who it was talking, his eyes pinned to the crumbling ceiling. There were definite footsteps. Someone was coming down the stairs.

"Chuck? Tim?" Frank called out, hoping against hope the guys were finally back. Maybe they'd all have a laugh about it, and Frank could punch both of them for getting everyone so worried. He knew it wasn't going to happen, though.

Whatever was coming down the stairs wasn't friendly. He just knew it.

The men had their flashlights aimed at the bottom couple of steps they could see. No one moved or made a sound.

Frank took out his phone and began filming. He didn't know why but figured it might be important. The footsteps stopped just above their line of sight.

One of the men took a step forward, craning his neck to see around the cement wall.

That's when the attack came from all sides.

The sound of running feet behind Frank made him turn and he sucked in a breath.

Creatures. That's all he could call them. Black, hairy and with insanely long talons on hands and feet. Two were coming through the doorway while others hopped through the gaps where the windows had been. Others were crawling on the ceiling and had already passed where he was standing.

The ceiling creatures dropped into the group, claws slashing.

It was utter chaos.

Frank wasn't sure who it was, but someone had a gun. The first shot was unexpected and so loud he thought his eardrum had been shattered. He fell to the ground, which saved him from a raking talon where his head had been a second ago. The creature jumped over his body.

The doorway was clear for a second, and Frank took advantage. He crawled until he was able to stop panicking and get to his feet, rushing out into the darkness.

His phone and flashlight were gone. Had he dropped them? Right now all he cared about was getting as far away as possible.

If he could get to the gate and hide on the small landing, maybe he'd have a chance before he was found. Hiro might be on his way, and he'd jump in the water and swim if he had to. Sharks be damned.

Frank heard the screams and more gunshots. He peeked through the gate and wished he hadn't. A couple of the men were running, pursued by the creatures. There must've been fifty of them, all swarming.

No, Frank thought. *Not swarming. Funneling them down the street. Leading their victims into a specific area.*

He lost track of the men as their flashlight beams were blocked by buildings, but he heard the cries.

Frank looked out to the water, praying he'd see a light for a boat, but with the shoreline's buildings glowing brightly, it was hard to know what was heading in his direction.

Of course, once it grew dark, the many fishing boats anchored off the island had gone back to their docks for the night. They'd return in the morning. Frank wondered if any of them would be alive by then.

He couldn't see anything when he turned back to the gate. Without a flashlight or phone, he was blind. The moon didn't offer enough light to see much, but then he saw it: movement. Blackness within the blackness, moving right at him.

Frank knew staying on this five foot by five foot slab with the water on three sides was no longer an option. The creatures had night vision and could see him.

Because they're from the mine, Frank thought.

Instead of rushing the gate, they seemed to be holding back. They couldn't be afraid of the water. He had no doubt they'd sunk the boat and killed the captain.

"What if I don't play this game and come out? Will you attack me then?" Frank asked, feeling like he was losing his mind.

He didn't hear anything but knew the creatures were watching. Waiting.

Frank took another look back but still couldn't tell if anyone was coming. The noise in his ears from his panic wasn't helping, either. He couldn't hear a motor if it was a few feet away.

He opened the gate fully, expecting to be attacked. Frank took a few steps forward and heard the gate slam shut behind him. He didn't need to turn to know they'd already surrounded him.

"Time to run," Frank said, knowing it was futile. Was this a fun game for the creatures? "You shouldn't play with your food." He was losing his mind as he began to run in the direction the others had gone, knowing it was the only route he'd be allowed to go.

Frank nearly tripped a couple of times in the street, hoping he'd nudged a stray chunk of cement block and not a fallen friend.

He heard another scream and a gunshot in the distance.

The way he was going.

Toward certain death.

Frank turned to his right, cutting a sharp corner, and headed into the closest building.

He ran up the stairs to the next level, turned and followed the steps up and up.

They were in pursuit.

At the top floor, Frank ran out of space.

The wall overlooking the water had been knocked out, giving him a clear view of Nagasaki in the distance as well as the boat approaching.

His way off the island, seven stories below and a million miles away.

Frank had nothing to use to get their attention. His flashlight and phone were missing.

He didn't need to turn around to know the creatures were creeping closer. He imagined them on the walls and ceiling, getting closer inch by inch.

Frank hoped his wife would be taken care of. He prayed some of his men had escaped. Someday, someone might find his phone and see the video he'd filmed.

The world needed to know about Forbidden Island. The truth of what was happening.

Frank wasn't going to be the one to tell that story, though.

He turned and saw the red eyes of the creatures a few feet away. Cornering him.

Frank glanced back over his shoulder. Could he make the water? It would be a far swim to the landing and the boat. Sharks in the water.

"What else can I do. Right?" Frank turned and leapt out, wishing he'd had a running start.

The darkness covered his view from either the water or the island catching his fall.

Not that it mattered. Both would feel like concrete as he slammed into it.

Frank heard another gunshot before he felt an intense pain and faded to black.

CHAPTER 21

"You're not supposed to be onboard," Hiro said to Kris, who'd appeared out of nowhere as soon as they launched from the dock. "How did you get on the boat?"

"I have my ways," Kris said. She was dressed in tight jeans, a black t-shirt and work boots. Her hair was still done up, but she'd tied a bandanna to hold it in place.

Hiro shook his head. The woman was amazing. He wondered how much it would cost to lure her over to The Texan's side. It would cost a pretty penny but be worth it.

It was dark. So dark Hiro didn't see the island until they were nearly upon it. There were no lights. Just an empty rock.

He had three men with him, all quiet killers who The Texan had procured from his personal contacts. Hiro thought it overkill to have assassins, but he wasn't the boss.

As they began to pull up to the landing spot, Hiro heard gunshots.

So did the three men, who immediately drew weapons.

Kris had a pistol in her hand. He didn't bother asking where she'd gotten it, and how she'd smuggled it into the country. This woman was impressive.

As they neared the island a horrific noise from underneath the boat wailed, and the boat shook. Everyone fell to their knees.

"We hit something," the captain yelled. "I need to pull back and see the damage."

"Get off. Now. We need to find the men," Hiro said.

Hiro let the three men get onto steady ground first. They pushed the gate open and Hiro heard another gunshot.

Kris jumped next, just as the boat began to pull back.

Hiro looked at the widening gap. "Get me closer."

The captain shook his head. "There's a sunken ship blocking the way."

"Then I'll take the dinghy." Hiro shook his head at Kris, who was standing on the landing. The three men had already gone onto the island. He didn't hear gunshots yet, which might be a good thing.

Kris gave him a wave and went through the gate before he could tell her to wait for him.

Hiro told the captain he'd give him double if he could get close enough for Hiro to jump onto the landing. It would take too long to get the small boat out and ready, and he didn't want to row with the current sloshing against the island.

The captain looked like he was going to refuse, but he finally nodded.

"Close as I can get," the captain yelled as he pushed the boat closer. "Lucky the hull didn't rip already."

Hiro stood on the rail of the boat and jumped.

For a second, he thought he'd make it safely, until gravity gripped his body and tossed him into the side of the landing, where he reached out his arms and thought they were going to be ripped from their sockets.

The pain was intense but he managed to hang on, his legs in the water.

Hiro pulled himself onto the landing and sat up.

The boat was already moving away with the tide, and the captain had his spotlight in the water.

Hiro was shaking when he saw the sharks just under the water, a second too late to make him a late-night snack.

"I'll dock out a bit," the captain yelled. "Let me know when you need a ride."

Hiro stood. He needed to catch up with his team.

There was a splash in the water nearby, but it was too far and too dark to see.

"Find out what that was," Hiro yelled to the captain. He was stalling and he knew it.

With a large flashlight in one hand and a pistol in the other, Hiro went through the gate and took stock of the horror scene before him: blood on the ground. What might be a part of someone's arm and hand on a block of cement. Distant screams.

He heard rapid fire gunshots. Probably the men he'd brought with him. Whoever was on the island was getting pushed back, because the noises were in the distance. Even as small as the island was, it sounded like a mile away. The sounds had a weird way of bouncing around the buildings.

A dark shape ran just out of the flashlight beam range, and Hiro tried to follow, but whatever it was had been too fast.

Were they dealing with an attack by a rival? A group of mercenaries dropped onto the island to wipe out the workers and create a problem for The Texan? Was it something else completely? Hiro would never presume what it was in public, but he had his own private thoughts.

His gut told him this wasn't a hostile corporate takeover shot, a move to discredit The Texan and take the island. This was something else.

He wondered where Kris had gone off to. It didn't seem safe to have her alone, even though she was tough. The paid men weren't going to protect her. They were hired to save the workers and kill anyone else. Clean up this mess before it gets any bigger, whatever this mess truly was.

More movement just out of range to either side. Hiro spun around, expecting to be attacked from behind. There was only rubble and darkness.

A crunch of rock to his left, as if someone were running on the ground.

Hiro turned and stared dumbly at what he was seeing.

It was the size of a small boy. Hairy. Black fur. Red eyes. Teeth so big they were sticking from the overlarge mouth. Claws on the hands and feet that looked deadly.

Hiro took a step back and heard an approach from behind as well.

He turned and fired, the shot slicing through another creature's neck. With a splash of blood and a groan, it fell to the ground.

They can be killed, whatever they are, Hiro thought. He intended to kill as many as he could and hoped the men he'd hired took care of the rest. How many of them could there be, anyway? The island was small.

Hiro spun around to shoot but the original creature he'd seen was gone. He listened but didn't hear anything. He started to walk, scanning the area all around with the light as he moved. He didn't want to trip or be ambushed.

The Texan would need a full report, and Hiro thought the most prudent move would be to close off the island. Figure out where these things were hiding. What they were.

He heard noises behind him, but when he turned, they kept moving back. He was definitely being stalked. Followed just out of range.

Pushing him forward. They might be bloodthirsty monsters, but they had an animal cunning. They were blocking three of four directions, forcing him to keep moving down the street, where the others had gone.

There weren't any more gunshots, which was distressing. It should mean the enemy had been destroyed, but Hiro knew it meant something far worse.

His beam touched a body on the ground and he stopped.

The creatures grunted behind him in the distance, as if telling him to keep moving forward to death.

It was one of the hired assassins on the ground. His stomach and throat had been ripped open, his flesh in pieces in the dirt.

Hiro ran to him and scooped up his weapon, turning and firing. He heard a grunt and knew he'd connected with a creature.

How many were there if a shot in the dark could hit the mark?

The light showed him the answer as at least twenty of them approached, most of them clinging to the building walls with their claws.

Hiro began shooting until both weapons were empty. He'd killed a few but not nearly enough.

As he turned to find another downed man and another weapon, he smelled the creatures. Inches from where he stood. A dozen of them.

The first swipe of a claw eviscerated Hiro and he dropped his flashlight.

He'd never get to tell The Texan what was happening.

CHAPTER 22

It had taken longer than Akira wanted, and it was nearly noon by the time they had started the boat ride over to the island, two ships filled with hardened men and crates of weapons and explosives.

Akira wondered how many of them had a criminal record. He supposed most of them, and it made him question this move again and again. No one spoke. He didn't know how much information Eddie had given them. Likely the money talked instead.

"We'll put you onto the island with the small boats," the captain said. He pointed at the sunken boat blocking the landing.

Akira wanted to be in the first boat, but Eddie talked him down. "It's better we get some of these men onto the island first. Let them set up a perimeter."

In short order, the boats were dropped into the water and it was less than fifty feet to get to the landing. Men disappeared through the gate.

Akira and Eddie went in the last boat, telling the captain to stay within sight.

The men hadn't gone far, checking weapons and keeping an eye out.

Eddie took charge, telling the men to do a building to building search. They were looking for the workers on Forbidden Island and whatever was keeping them here.

Akira called out for Kris, knowing she was here, too. She hadn't answered his phone calls.

They began searching two buildings at once on either side of the street, moving in a definite pattern. Sweeping across the small island, weapons ready.

"We have something," one of the men called out. Everyone immediately stopped and dropped, weapons scanning where they hadn't gone to yet.

Akira and Eddie, who'd been following behind, came up and inspected the trail of blood. It led through the center of the island between the buildings.

"I'll bet you it stops at the mine," Akira said. He'd read so much about the island on the plane ride, and knew the problems stemmed from the mine. Where they'd surmised a collapse or an explosion was the culprit for the mass evacuation, Akira thought it was something... supernatural? Unknown. He had an open mind. Maybe it was a deadly gas or a mutant animal.

Instead of rushing to the mine, Akira told the men to keep sweeping but do it quickly. The goal was the mine entrance.

He helped with the search despite Eddie's protests. It would get done sooner with every man pitching in, and Eddie finally relented and began helping as well.

Akira looked out over the water between the island and the coastline and saw dozens of fishing boats anchored. He knew they were being watched. The cat was out of the bag, and if unconfirmed reports were true, there'd been gunfire here last night. Based on the blood trails, it seemed more than likely everyone who'd been on the island was now dead.

Dragged to the mine.

The buildings offered no more clues. They stood at the mine entrance. The thick metal door was welded shut, but one of the men found a small side entrance that could be opened.

"I want half the team inside and half out. We're going to blow this from within and part of the structure around it so it collapses and there's no chance of anything coming or going," Akira said.

"Anything? What's down there?" one of the men asked.

Akira wasn't going to lie. "Something really dangerous. I need a small team to go down with me and look for survivors. Well-armed men."

"Akira, no. I'll do it," Eddie said. "You need to organize the demolition."

"They know what they're doing." Akira pointed at six men. "Follow me."

"You have forty-five minutes," the crew chief said. "We'll be ready to blow."

"If you don't hear from us in ninety minutes… proceed," Akira said. "Or if there's a major problem."

"Like what?"

"You'll know." Akira led with his flashlight, entering the main tunnel. The men spread out around him, weapons drawn and ready. They had their own flashlights and kept them at an angle so twenty feet in front of the group was bathed in light.

They followed the path down, stray rail ties and rotting wooden beams everywhere.

"I see a lot of footprints," Eddie said. "Not all of them human."

Most of them weren't human, too small and deformed. They could see claw marks up and down the walls, too. Even the ceiling. No one commented, but Akira knew everyone was on edge and ready for anything.

It came just as they passed through a cluster of wooden beams piled on the sides, forming a natural funnel through the tunnel.

It was a trap, forcing them to move one at a time.

The creatures rushed the first couple of men through the gap, ripping them apart with claws and fangs. The monsters were pushed back with gunfire, killing half a dozen before they retreated back into the darkness.

"What are they?" Eddie asked.

"Whatever they are, they're smart. They waited until we were in this spot before attacking," Akira said. He stooped down and looked at the creature. The smell was unbearable this close to it. A musk like sweat, unwashed flesh and coal dust. "Let's keep going but watch for the next attack." He took a fallen man's weapon and handed another to Eddie.

The next attack came as the tunnel forked to the left and right. A dozen creatures attacked from both tunnels, crawling on the ceiling, walls and running on the floor.

Gunshots exploded, Akira covering his ears. They were still ringing from the last attack, and he wondered if he'd lose part of his hearing and if there would be more shots. More bloodshed.

The creatures took heavy losses and retreated down the tunnels.

"Which way?" Eddie yelled, his hearing impaired as well.

"No way we split up." Akira looked at the men for any idea, but they simply followed orders. "We leave two men here and the rest of us go to the right." There were only two men left with Akira and Eddie. He knew they should pull back, but they'd only been searching a few minutes.

They proceeded with even more caution. The tunnels branched off multiple times but they kept straight.

It was well-worn with traffic on the floor and walls. How many of these creatures were down here? It might be a vast underground city for them. Hundreds. Thousands. What did they eat? How come no one had seen them above ground during the day? Akira knew they hated the light. The flashlights seemed to blind them, and they attacked wildly, aiming at the lights more than the humans, overwhelming with sheer numbers.

Akira had one man in front of him. The next attack came just as the man crossed through an intersection, a creature falling from a gap above and rending the man's chest and neck with claws that dug deep. Akira shot the creature but several more fell from the ceiling and rushed him.

Eddie was firing next to Akira, hitting the mark each time and killing a monster.

But there were too many.

The other man with them was firing as well, and he stepped into the tunnel to the right as more of them entered the fight.

Eddie fired until his weapon was empty, throwing it at a creature inches from ripping Akira's neck with a claw. "We need to go back."

Akira turned. Dozens of creatures were jammed into the tunnel behind them.

"Run," Eddie said. Akira shot two monsters right before they skewered Eddie, but when he ran out of bullets they fell upon Eddie. He was lost in the dark pile, his flashlight crushed.

Akira ran. He couldn't see where he was going, taking turns at random and knowing they were right behind him.

They began to groan and screech, their claws clicking against the hard walls of coal.

"Mom? Dad? Are you down here? Is anyone down here?" Akira screamed and kept running.

CHAPTER 23

Kimiko was taking charge, even if it killed her. She was weak. The meager charred meat and dirty water was getting to her. She hadn't heard the creatures in hours, and her stomach was groaning. She knew it was past meal time for her, and she silently prayed the creatures had either been killed or caught.

She flicked the lighter and panicked, because it didn't catch at first. She tried a dozen times before it caught, lighting her small room.

It looked smaller than it was, a natural pocket in the earth. Strange carvings littered the walls, ceiling and floor. She walked out, expecting to be attacked.

There were muffled noises in the distance but she had no idea how far they were or what was causing it.

Kimiko followed the natural hallway and looked inside the surrounding rooms.

She stopped and put a hand over her mouth, nearly dropping the lighter.

The remains of Daisuke were piled in the middle of a chamber, his body ripped apart. Only his face remained untouched, as if they had taken care of his head as they ravaged him.

Kimiko wanted to cry. Here was her husband, a man who had taken care of her. Who had done horrible things to her and their son. A man who was the greatest and worst person she'd ever met.

Dead. Gone.

There were other bodies in other rooms. Men she didn't know. They looked freshly killed, too. They didn't smell of rot, although they would soon enough.

Unless I can escape, Kimiko thought.

With no idea where the exit was, she began to move down the hallway. Then she stopped. The lighter was hurting her finger and it had gone out a couple of times when her finger slipped.

Despite not wanting to touch a dead body, Kimiko steeled herself and did it. She found two flashlights that still worked and a pocketknife.

She needed to be strong. Survive this and get out of the mine. Kimiko took a deep breath, filled with coal dust, and started moving. As long as she kept moving, she'd be fine.

What if she was attacked? The pocketknife wasn't going to do much damage, but it was all she had.

Then she heard the call. It sounded like Akira, but… was it possible? Had she been down here so long, subsisting on rats and dirty water, she'd become delusional?

No. She heard him again, closer.

Kimiko didn't know whether to call out and perhaps give away her position or wait to see if he came closer. *It's Akira, you idiot*, she thought. *He's come to save you.*

She began to call out his name, expecting the creatures at any moment to find her first.

Akira shouted back and they had several rounds, Kimiko staying in place. The words echoed and it was hard to tell from which direction Akira was coming from.

A light bobbed at the other end of the corridor and Kimiko wanted to cry with joy. It was Akira. He saw her but didn't stop running, waving at her to go. Run. Flee.

Kimiko saw why, as a horde of creatures was on his tail.

She knew there was nowhere to run. She hadn't found an escape route, only a few rooms with dead bodies. And her husband.

She backtracked quickly to where Daisuke was laid out. She didn't want to die in the room she'd been held captive. It felt like giving up. At least here, with her family, she could die in peace.

Akira followed, turning in the doorway and shining his light into the creature's eyes. They backed away and kept a respectable distance.

"I have a lighter," Kimiko said.

Akira gasped when he saw his father.

"I'm so sorry, son," she said. She was crying. "I did my best but it wasn't good enough. He loved you in his own way. You know that. Right? He was very proud of you, even though you opposed his work. He collected all of your press. He had articles about you printed out and put into files. He kept me abreast of what you were doing."

Akira was still staring at his father. "Then why was he so awful to me?"

Kimiko opened her mouth to answer but hesitated. "I don't really know. He loved you so much but when you were around… I begged him to stop alienating you, son."

The creatures grunted in the corridor.

"We're not getting out of here," Akira said. "Unless you know a secret route."

Kimiko shook her head.

Akira stripped the bloody shirt off of his father. "Give me the lighter. Maybe we can force our way out."

He lit the shirt and went to the door, waving it at the creatures. They moved back a few steps but didn't retreat. Kimiko could see they weren't going to leave them alone. Some of them had crawled on the ceiling and gotten down the other side of the corridor, too. They were trapped in this room now.

Akira left the burning clothing in the doorway and hugged his mother. "I missed you."

"Will they come to rescue us?"

Akira squeezed her tighter. "No. They'll blow the mine. Cave it in. Hopefully stop these monsters from escaping and hurting anyone else." He let her go and sat with his back to the wall, his father between him and the doorway.

Kimiko joined him, her fingers intertwined in his. ,

"How do they survive? How many are there? What are they?" Akira asked.

"They breed rats, I think. It's what I've been living on," Kimiko said. "They even cooked them for me. They're smarter than they look. I have no idea how many there are, but they can see in darkness."

The fire was out. Kimiko wondered how long Akira's flashlight would hold up. A few of the creatures sat down in the doorway and silently watched them.

"The Texan wanted to turn this island into an amusement park for the rich," Akira said. "He even renamed it Kimiko Island in your honor."

She laughed. "Your father would've liked that. The renaming part, not the fact The Texan took it and wanted to use it for his own amusement."

Akira was looking at the ceiling. "I wonder if it will all collapse on us, or if we'll just be trapped with them."

Kimiko stared at the creatures. She tapped her mouth and grunted like she'd heard them do. One of them stood and ran off. "I think I ordered cooked rat and coal water for lunch."

"We could rush them. See how many we can take out before they kill us," Akira said.

"Or we wait. We see what happens." Kimiko closed her eyes and snuggled next to her son. If she were going to die, this was the best possible scenario for her. "We have a lot of catching up to do, too. A lot of apologies I need to make."

"You don't owe me anything, mother."

A distant rumble filled the air, and the creatures looked irritated, beginning to stand.

"They're doing what I paid them to do," Akira said. "Seal off the mine."

Some dust fell from the ceiling but it didn't collapse. A series of rumbles shook the ground they were sitting on but nothing more.

After a few seconds it went quiet.

"I think we're trapped," Akira said. He sighed. "I don't feel panicked or scared, though. Is that weird?"

Kimiko hugged her son. "No. I feel the same way. I love you, Akira. I'm sorry…"

Akira shook his head. "If they wanted to kill us, we'd be dead already. I don't want to know what they have in mind."

Neither did Kimiko. She'd enjoy her time with her son as long as she could.

The flashlight started to fade.

CHAPTER 24

The Texan hung up the phone and put his feet up on the desk, his boots scattering his papers.

Was this salvageable?

His relatives were outside messing with his horses again. He went to dial Hiro and frowned. The man was one of the missing. His body had never been recovered. The only body had been Frank Meyer, or what was left of it after the sharks had finished.

Akira was missing. His parents were still missing. There'd been an explosion on Kimiko Island. The mine had collapsed, taking five buildings with it. A large break in the structure of the island itself had occurred.

The government could no longer turn a blind eye, and The Texan knew no amount of money was going to save it.

Best to walk away and chalk up the loss, he thought.

He wasn't heartless. He'd liked Hiro. He'd miss the man, too. It had taken him many years to find someone who understood his goals and carried out the smallest of tasks as if it were so important.

It wouldn't be long before the phone calls began. He'd need to get in front of this chaos. Figure out a solution that made him look like the good guy.

The Texan stood and went to the window, watching the idiot kin trying to ride his prized possessions like... well, like idiots. He closed his eyes.

"This is a tragedy of epic proportions. If I'd known there was any chance, any at all, something could or would happen on Kimiko Island, rest assured, I would have done something about it. All safety protocol was used. All. I am going to personally make sure anyone missing will be found, and families will be compensated..."

"I wouldn't say that. It makes you sound guilty, which you are."

The Texan turned to see Kris Scarlet, wearing a tight black dress and heels, standing in his office doorway.

"How'd you get in? I have security," The Texan said.

Kris smiled. "It is one of my many talents." She went to his bar and poured herself a generous helping of his bourbon. "Care for one?"

The Texan sat down in his chair and smiled. "Yes, but those bottles are for guests. Not the best stuff. There's a twenty-three year Pappy Van Winkle underneath, behind the Maker's Mark. Pour yourself one, too, ma'am."

Kris downed the glass before finding the bottle of Pappy and pouring them both a helping. She brought them to the desk, a smile on her face, and sat down.

"What can I do for you?" The Texan wondered what she knew. She was in Nagasaki. She might even have gone to the island. How had she escaped?

As if reading his mind, Kris put down her glass. "I got off the island. In the confusion, with the men Hiro hired getting torn apart, I went back to the gate and waved the boat over. The captain took me back to the mainland, where I promptly got as far away as possible."

"And Hiro?"

Kris shrugged. "Dead. I saw him die. He seemed like a good man."

"What happened to Akira and his team?" The Texan knew Akira had hired not only a group of thugs but an explosives crew. He was sure they'd blown up the entrance to the mine.

"I don't know. By the time I got far enough away, I tried calling him. He never answered." She finally stopped smiling. "He was on the island. He's gone."

"Then you might be the sole survivor," The Texan said. He was getting nervous. What did she want besides a payoff?

Kris opened her small purse and took out a phone. "Frank, your foreman, dropped this. It was recovered by someone for a hefty cost." She put it on the desk. "It shows a video of the creatures that killed everyone."

"Why give it to me?"

"I'm not interested in the island. In fact, I'm here to make sure you leave it alone. Let it rot in the sun," Kris said. "At some point, when this all dies down, we can quietly go in and recover whatever needs to be recovered inside the mine."

"What do you want? How much?"

She shrugged again. "I will soon own all of Akira's assets." Now she was smiling again. "I got pretty good at forging his name back when we dated. Despite what he thought, I was never one of his father's many women. It was a professional relationship. It was love, yes, but it was also about the power and the money." She stood. "You'll find I'm going to be the new head of his company. The lawyers have already put it all into motion. Now... we can either join forces and work together, forming an alliance, or we can go to war over ego. It's up to you."

The Texan smiled. "I'll be in touch and let you know. I'm sure you can find your way out."

Kris drank down the bourbon and left without another word.

He knew he'd need to be careful with her. She was cunning. She was going to be trouble.

But that's for another day, he thought. *I still need to figure out how many men it will take to clear the island, open up the mine and clean it out, and begin plans for my adult amusement park. It will be a private island. No rules. No laws. I just need time for the smoke to clear.*

The Texan put his booted feet back on his desk and took a sip of his drink.

END

www.ingramcontent.com/pod-product-compliance
Lightning Source LLC
Chambersburg PA
CBHW051953170626
46808CB00007B/2602